EVIL UNDER THE SUN

AGATHA CHRISTIE is known throughout the world as the Queen of Crime. Her seventy-seven detective novels and books of stories have been translated into every major language, and her sales are calculated in tens of millions.

She began writing at the end of the First World War, when she created Hercule Poirot, the little Belgian detective with the egg-shaped head and the passion for order – the most popular sleuth in fiction since Sherlock Holmes. Poirot, fluffy Miss Marple and her other detectives have appeared in films, radio programmes and stage plays based on her books.

Agatha Christie also wrote six romantic novels under the pseudonym Mary Westmacott, several plays and a book of poems; as well, she assisted her archaeologist husband Sir Max Mallowan on many expeditions to the Near East.

Postern of Fate was the last book she wrote before her death in 1976, but since its publication two books Agatha Christie wrote in the 1940s have appeared: *Curtain: Poirot's Last Case* and *Sleeping Murder*, the last Miss Marple book. Agatha Christie's *Autobiography* was published in 1977.

AGATHA CHRISTIE

Evil
Under the Sun

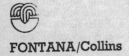

FONTANA/Collins

First published in 1941 by William Collins Sons & Co Ltd
First issued in Fontana Books 1957
Twentieth Impression July 1980

© 1940, 1941 by Agatha Christie

Made and printed in Great Britain by
William Collins Sons & Co Ltd Glasgow

TO JOHN

*In memory of our last season
in Syria*

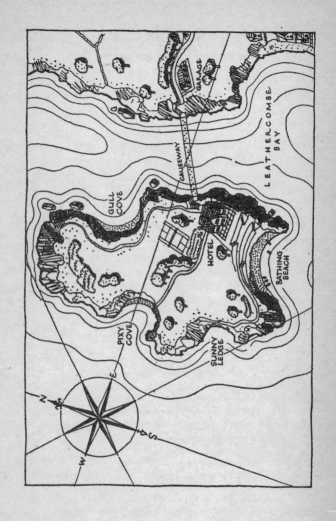

Chapter One

1

WHEN Captain Roger Angmering built himself a house in the year 1782 on the island off Leathercombe Bay, it was thought the height of eccentricity on his part. A man of good family such as he was should have had a decorous mansion set in wide meadows with, perhaps, a running stream and good pasture.

But Captain Roger Angmering had only one great love, the sea. So he built his house—a sturdy house too, as it needed to be, on the little windswept gull-haunted promontory—cut off from land at each high tide.

He did not marry, the sea was his first and last spouse, and at his death the house and island went to a distant cousin. That cousin and his descendants thought little of the bequest. Their own acres dwindled, and their heirs grew steadily poorer.

In 1922 when the great cult of the Seaside for Holidays was finally established and the coast of Devon and Cornwall was no longer thought too hot in the summer, Arthur Angmering found his vast inconvenient late Georgian house unsaleable, but he got a good price for the odd bit of property acquired by the seafaring Captain Roger.

The sturdy house was added to and embellished. A concrete causeway was laid down from the mainland to the island. "Walks" and "Nooks" were cut and devised all round the island. There were two tennis courts, sun-terraces leading down to a little bay embellished with rafts and diving boards. The Jolly Roger Hotel, Smugglers' Island, Leathercombe Bay, came triumphantly into being. And from June till September (with a short season at Easter) the Jolly Roger Hotel was usually packed to the attics. It was enlarged and improved in 1934 by the addition of a cocktail bar, a bigger dining-room and some extra bathrooms. The prices went up.

People said:

"Ever been to Leathercombe Bay? Awfully jolly hotel

7

there, on a sort of island. Very comfortable and no trippers
or charabancs. Good cooking and all that. You ought to go."

And people did go.

2

There was one very important person (in his own estima-
tion at least) staying at the Jolly Roger. Hercule Poirot,
resplendent in a white duck suit, with a panama hat tilted over
his eyes, his moustaches magnificently befurled, lay back in
an improved type of deck-chair and surveyed the bathing
beach. A series of terraces led down to it from the hotel.
On the beach itself were floats, lilos, rubber and canvas boats,
balls and rubber toys. There was a long springboard and three
rafts at varying distances from the shore.

Of the bathers, some were in the sea, some were lying
stretched out in the sun, and some were anointing themselves
carefully with oil.

On the terrace immediately above, the non-bathers sat and
commented on the weather, the scene in front of them, the
news in the morning papers and any other subject that
appealed to them.

On Poirot's left a ceaseless flow of conversation poured in
a gentle monotone from the lips of Mrs. Gardener while at the
same time her needles clacked as she knitted vigorously. Beyond her, her husband, Odell C. Gardener, lay in a hammock
chair, his hat tilted forward over his nose, and occasionally
uttered a brief statement when called upon to do so.

On Poirot's right, Miss Brewster, a tough athletic woman
with grizzled hair and a pleasant weather-beaten face, made
gruff comments. The result sounded rather like a sheepdog
whose short stentorian barks interrupted the ceaseless yapping
of a Pomeranian.

Mrs. Gardener was saying:

"And so I said to Mr. Gardener, why, I said, sight-seeing
is all very well, and I do like to do a place thoroughly.
But, after all, I said, we've done England pretty well and all
I want now is to get to some quiet spot by the seaside and just
relax. That's what I said, wasn't it, Odell? Just *relax*. I feel
I must relax, I said. That's so, isn't it, Odell?"

Mr. Gardner, from behind his hat, murmured:

" Yes, darling."

Mrs. Gardener pursued the theme.

" And so, when I mentioned it to Mr. Kelso, at Cook's— He's arranged all our itinerary for us and been *most* helpful in every way. I don't really know what we'd have done without him!—well, as I say, when I mentioned it to him, Mr. Kelso said that we couldn't do better than come here. A most picturesque spot, he said, quite out of the world, and at the same time very comfortable and most exclusive in every way. And, of course, Mr. Gardener, he chipped in there and said what about the sanitary arrangements? Because, if you'll believe me, M. Poirot, a sister of Mr. Gardener's went to stay at a guesthouse once, very exclusive they said it was, and in the heart of the moors, but would you believe me, *nothing but an earth closet!* So naturally that made Mr. Gardener suspicious of these out-of-the-world places, didn't it, Odell?"

" Why, yes, darling," said Mr. Gardener.

" But Mr. Kelso reassured us at once. The sanitation, he said, was absolutely the latest word, and the cooking was excellent. And I'm sure that's so. And what I like about it is, it's *intime,* if you know what I mean. Being a small place we all talk to each other and everybody knows everybody. If there is a fault about the British it is that they're inclined to be a bit stand-offish until they've known you a couple of years. After that nobody could be nicer. Mr. Kelso said that interesting people came here, and I see he was right. There's you, M. Poirot and Miss Darnley. Oh! I was just tickled to death when I found out who you were, wasn't I, Odell?"

" You were, darling."

" Ha!" said Miss Brewster, breaking in explosively. " What a thrill, eh, M. Poirot?"

Hercule Poirot raised his hands in deprecation. But it was no more than a polite gesture. Mrs. Gardener flowed smoothly on.

" You see, M. Poirot, I'd heard a lot about you from Cornelia Robson who was. Mr. Gardener and I were at Badenhof in May. And of course Cornelia told us all about that business in Egypt when Linnet Ridgeway was killed. She said you were wonderful and I've always been simply crazy to meet you, haven't I, Odell?"

" Yes, darling."

" And then Miss Darnley, too. I get a lot of my things at Rose Mond's and of course she *is* Rose Mond, isn't she? I think her clothes are ever so clever. Such a marvellous line. That dress I had on last night was one of hers. She's just a lovely woman in every way, I think."

From beyond Miss Brewster, Major Barry, who had been sitting with protuberant eyes glued to the bathers, grunted out:

" Distinguished lookin' gal!"

Mrs. Gardener clacked her needles.

" I've just got to confess one thing, M. Poirot. It gave me a kind of a *turn* meeting you here—not that I wasn't just thrilled to meet you, because I was. Mr. Gardener knows that. But it just came to me that you might be here—well, *professionally*. You know what I mean? Well, I'm just terribly sensitive, as Mr. Gardener will tell you, and I just couldn't bear it if I was to be mixed up in crime of any kind. You see——"

Mr. Gardener cleared his throat. He said:

" You see, M. Poirot, Mrs. Gardener is very sensitive."

The hands of Hercule Poirot shot into the air.

" But let me assure you, Madame, that I am here simply in the same way that you are here yourselves—to enjoy myself—to spend the holiday. I do not think of crime even."

Miss Brewster said again, giving her short gruff bark:

" No bodies on Smugglers' Island."

Hercule Poirot said:

" Ah! but that, it is not strictly true." He pointed downward. " Regard them there, lying out in rows. What are they? They are not men and women. There is nothing personal about them. They are just—bodies!"

Major Barry said appreciatively:

" Good-looking fillies, some of 'em. Bit on the thin side, perhaps."

Poirot cried:

" Yes, but what appeal is there? What mystery? I, I am old, of the old school. When I was young, one saw barely the ankle. The glimpse of a foamy petticoat, how alluring! The gentle swelling of the calf—a knee—a beribboned garter——"

" Naughty, naughty!" said Major Barry hoarsely.

" Much more sensible—the things we wear nowadays," said Miss Brewster.

"Why, yes, M. Poirot," said Mrs. Gardener. "I do think, you know, that our girls and boys nowadays lead a much more natural healthy life. They just romp about together and they—well, they—Mrs. Gardener blushed slightly for she had a nice mind—"they think nothing *of* it, if you know what I mean?"

"I do know," said Hercule Poirot. "It is deplorable!"

"Deplorable?" squeaked Mrs. Gardener.

"To remove all the romance—all the mystery! To-day everything is *standardised*!" He waved a hand towards the recumbent figures. "That reminds me very much of the Morgue in Paris."

"M. Poirot!" Mrs. Gardener was scandalised.

"Bodies—arranged on slabs—like butcher's meat!"

"But M. Poirot, isn't that too far-fetched for words?"

Hercule Poirot admitted:

"It may be, yes."

"All the same," Mrs. Gardener knitted with energy, "I'm inclined to agree with you on one point. These girls that lie out like that in the sun will grow hair on their legs and arms. I've said so to Irene—that's my daughter, M. Poirot. Irene, I said to her, if you lie out like that in the sun, you'll have hair all over you, hair on your arms and hair on your legs and hair on your bosom, and what will you look like then? I said to her. Didn't I, Odell?"

"Yes, darling," said Mr. Gardener.

Every one was silent, perhaps making a mental picture of Irene when the worst had happened.

Mrs. Gardener rolled up her knitting and said:

"I wonder now——"

Mr. Gardener said:

"Yes, darling?"

He struggled out of the hammock chair and took Mrs. Gardener's knitting and her book. He asked:

"What about joining us for a drink, Miss Brewster?"

"Not just now, thanks."

The Gardeners went up to the hotel.

Miss Brewster said:

"American husbands are wonderful!"

3

Mrs. Gardener's place was taken by the Reverend Stephen Lane.

Mr. Lane was a tall vigorous clergyman of fifty odd. His face was tanned and his dark grey flannel trousers were holidayfied and disreputable.

He said with enthusiasm:

"Marvellous country! I've been from Leathercombe Bay to Harford and back over the cliffs."

"Warm work walking to-day," said Major Barry who never walked.

"Good exercise," said Miss Brewster. "I haven't been for my row yet. Nothing like rowing for your stomach muscles."

The eyes of Hercule Poirot dropped somewhat ruefully to a certain protuberance in his middle.

Miss Brewster, noting the glance, said kindly:

"You'd soon get that off, M. Poirot, if you took a rowing-boat out every day."

"*Merci, Mademoiselle.* I detest boats!"

"You mean small boats?"

"Boats of all sizes!" He closed his eyes and shuddered. "The movement of the sea, it is not pleasant."

"Bless the man, the sea is as calm as a mill pond to-day."

Poirot replied with conviction:

"There is no such thing as a really calm sea. Always, always, there is motion."

"If you ask me," said Major Barry, "seasickness is nine-tenths nerves."

"There," said the clergyman, smiling a little, "speaks the good sailor—eh, Major?"

"Only been ill once—and that was crossing the Channel! Don't think about it, that's my motto."

"Seasickness is really a very odd thing," mused Miss Brewster. "Why should some people be subject to it and not others? It seems so unfair. And nothing to do with one's ordinary health. Quite sickly people are good sailors. Someone told me once it was something to do with one's spine. Then there's the way some people can't stand heights. I'm not very good myself, but Mrs. Redfern is far worse. The other day, on the cliff path to Harford, she turned quite giddy and simply clung to me. She told me she once got stuck halfway down that outside staircase on Milan Cathedral. She'd gone up without thinking but coming down did for her."

"She'd better not go down the ladder to Pixy Cove, then," observed Lane.

Miss Brewster made a face.

"I funk that myself. It's all right for the young. The Cowan boys and the young Mastermans, they run up and down it and enjoy it."

Lane said:

"Here comes Mrs. Redfern now, coming up from her bathe."

Miss Brewster remarked:

"M. Poirot ought to approve of her. She's no sun-bather."

Young Mrs. Redfern had taken off her rubber cap and was shaking out her hair. She was an ash blonde and her skin was of that dead fairness that goes with that colouring. Her legs and arms were very white.

With a hoarse chuckle, Major Barry said:

"Looks a bit uncooked among the others, doesn't she?"

Wrapping herself in a long bath-robe Christine Redfern came up the beach and mounted the steps towards them.

She had a fair serious face, pretty in a negative way and small dainty hands and feet.

She smiled at them and dropped down beside them, tucking her bath-wrap round her.

Miss Brewster said:

"You have earned M. Poirot's good opinion. He doesn't like the sun-tanning crowd. Says they're like joints of butcher's meat, or words to that effect."

Christine Redfern smiled ruefully. She said:

"I wish I *could* sun-bathe! But I don't go brown. I only blister and get the most frightful freckles all over my arms."

"Better than getting hair all over them like Mrs. Gardener's Irene," said Miss Brewster. In answer to Christine's inquiring glance she went on: "Mrs. Gardener's been in grand form this morning. Absolutely non-stop. 'Isn't that so, Odell?' 'Yes, darling.'" She paused and then said: "I wish, though, M. Poirot, that you'd played up to her a bit. Why didn't you? Why didn't you tell her that you were down here investigating a particularly gruesome murder, and that the murderer, a homicidal maniac, was certainly to be found among the guests of the hotel?"

Hercule Poirot sighed. He said:

"I very much fear she would have believed me."

Major Barry gave a wheezy chuckle. He said:

"She certainly would."

Emily Brewster said:

"No, I don't believe even Mrs. Gardener would have believed in a crime staged here. This isn't the sort of place you'd get a body!"

Hercule Poirot stirred a little in his chair. He protested. He said:

"But why not, Mademoiselle? Why should there not be what you call a 'body' here on Smugglers' Island?"

Emily Brewster said:

"I don't know. I suppose some places *are* more unlikely than others. This isn't the kind of spot——" She broke off, finding it difficult to explain her meaning.

"It is romantic, yes," agreed Hercule Poirot. "It is peaceful. The sun shines. The sea is blue. But you forget, Miss Brewster, there is evil everywhere under the sun."

The clergyman stirred in his chair. He leaned forward. His intensely blue eyes lighted up.

Miss Brewster shrugged her shoulders.

"Oh! of course I realise that, but all the same——"

"But all the same this still seems to you an unlikely setting for crime? You forget one thing, Mademoiselle."

"Human nature, I suppose?"

"That, yes. That, always. But that was not what I was going to say. I was going to point out to you that here every one is on holiday."

Emily Brewster turned a puzzled face to him.

"I don't understand."

Hercule Poirot beamed kindly at her. He made dabs in the air with an emphatic forefinger.

"Let us say, you have an enemy. If you seek him out in his flat, in his office, in the street—*eh bien*, you must have a *reason*—you must account for yourself. But here at the seaside it is necessary for no one to account for himself. You are at Leathercombe Bay, why? *Parbleu!* it is August —one goes to the seaside in August—one is on one's holiday. It is quite natural, you see, for you to be here and for Mr.

Lane to be here and for Major Barry to be here and for Mrs. Redfern and her husband to be here. Because it is the custom in England to go to the seaside in August."

"Well," admitted Miss Brewster, "that's certainly a very ingenious idea. But what about the Gardeners? They're American."

Poirot smiled.

"Even Mrs. Gardener, as she told us, feels the need to *relax*. Also, since she is 'doing' England, she must certainly spend a fortnight at the seaside—as a good tourist, if nothing else. She enjoys watching people."

Mrs. Redfern murmured:

"You like watching the people too, I think?"

"Madame I will confess it. I do."

She said thoughtfully: "You see—a good deal."

4

There was a pause. Stephen Lane cleared his throat and said with a trace of self-consciousness.

"I was interested, M. Poirot, in something you said just now. You said that there was evil done everywhere under the sun. It was almost a quotation from Ecclesiastes." He paused and then quoted himself. "*Yea, also the heart of the sons of men is full of evil, and madness is in their heart while they live.*" His face lit up with an almost fanatical light. "I was glad to hear you say that. Nowadays, no one believes in evil. It is considered, at most, a mere negation of good. Evil, people say, is done by those who know no better—who are undeveloped—who are to be pitied rather than blamed. But M. Poirot, evil is *real*! It is a *fact*! I believe in Evil like I believe in Good. It exists! It is powerful! It walks the earth!"

He stopped. His breath was coming fast. He wiped his forehead with his handkerchief and looked suddenly apologetic.

"I'm sorry. I got carried away."

Poirot said calmly:

"I understand your meaning. Up to a point I agree with you. Evil does walk the earth and can be recognised as such."

Major Barry cleared his throat.

"Talking of that sort of thing, some of these fakir fellers in India——"

Major Barry had been long enough at the Jolly Roger for every one to be on their guard against his fatal tendency to embark on long Indian stories. Both Miss Brewster and Mrs. Redfern burst into speech.

"That's your husband swimming in now, isn't it, Mrs. Redfern? How magnificent his crawl stroke is. He's an awfully good swimmer."

At the same moment Mrs. Redfern said:

"Oh look! What a lovely little boat that is out there with the red sails. It's Mr. Blatt's, isn't it?"

The sailing boat with the red sails was just crossing the end of the bay.

Major Barry grunted:

"Fanciful idea, red sails," but the menace of the story about the fakir was avoided.

Hercule Poirot looked with appreciation at the young man who had just swum to shore. Patrick Redfern was a good specimen of humanity. Lean, bronzed with broad shoulders and narrow thighs, there was about him a kind of infectious enjoyment and gaiety—a native simplicity that endeared him to all women and most men.

He stood there shaking the water from him and raising a hand in gay salutation to his wife.

She waved back calling out:

"Come up here, Pat."

"I'm coming."

He went a little way along the beach to retrieve the towel he had left there.

It was then that a woman came down past them from the hotel to the beach.

Her arrival had all the importance of a stage entrance.

Moreover, she walked as though she knew it. There was no self-consciousness apparent. It would seem that she was too used to the invariable effect her presence produced.

She was tall and slender. She wore a simple backless white bathing dress and every inch of her exposed body was tanned a beautiful even shade of bronze. She was as perfect as a statue. Her hair was a rich flaming auburn curling richly and intimately into her neck. Her face had that slight hardness which is seen when thirty years have come and gone, but the whole effect of her was one of youth—of superb and triumphant vitality. There was a Chinese immobility about her face, and an upward slant of the dark blue eyes. On her head she wore a fantastic Chinese hat of jade green cardboard.

There was that about her which made every other woman on the beach seem faded and insignificant. And with equal inevitability, the eye of every male present was drawn and riveted on her.

The eyes of Hercule Poirot opened, his moustache quivered appreciatively, Major Barry sat up and his protuberant eyes bulged even farther with excitement; on Poirot's left the Reverend Stephen Lane drew in his breath with a little hiss and his figure stiffened.

Major Barry said in a hoarse whisper:

"Arlena Stuart (that's who she was before she married Marshall)—I saw her in *Come and Go* before she left the stage. Something worth looking at, eh?"

Christine Redfern said slowly and her voice was cold: "She's handsome—yes. I think—she looks rather a beast!"

Emily Brewster said abruptly:

"You talked about evil just now, M. Poirot. Now to my mind that woman's a personification of evil! She's a bad lot through and through. I happen to know a good deal about her."

Major Barry said reminiscently:

"I remember a gal out in Simla. *She* had red hair too. Wife of a subaltern. Did she set the place by the ears? I'll say she did! Men went mad about her! All the women, of course, would have liked to gouge her eyes out! She upset the apple cart in more homes than one."

He chuckled reminiscently.

"Husband was a nice quiet fellow. Worshipped the ground she walked on. Never saw a thing—or made out he didn't."

Stephen Lane said in a low voice full of intense feeling:

"Such women are a menace—a menace to——"

He stopped.

Arlena Stuart had come to the water's edge. Two young men, little more than boys, had sprung up and come eagerly towards her. She stood smiling at them.

Her eyes slid past them to where Patrick Redfern was coming along the beach.

It was, Hercule Poirot thought, like watching the needle of a compass. Patrick Redfern was deflected, his feet changed their direction. The needle, do what it will, must obey the law of magnetism and turn to the north. Patrick Redfern's feet brought him to Arlena Stuart.

She stood smiling at him. Then she moved slowly along the beach by the side of the waves. Patrick Redfern went with her. She stretched herself out by a rock. Redfern dropped to the shingle beside her.

Abruptly, Christine Redfern got up and went into the hotel.

5

There was an uncomfortable little silence after she had left. Then Emily Brewster said:

" It's rather too bad. She's a nice little thing. They've only been married a year or two."

" Gal I was speaking of," said Major Barry, " the one in Simla. She upset a couple of really happy marriages. Seemed a pity, what?"

" There's a type of woman," said Miss Brewster, " who *likes* smashing up homes." She added after a minute or two, " Patrick Redfern's a fool!"

Hercule Poirot said nothing. He was gazing down the beach, but he was not looking at Patrick Redfern and Arlena Stuart.

Miss Brewster said:

" Well, I'd better go and get hold of my boat."

She left them.

Major Barry turned his boiled gooseberry eyes with mild curiosity on Poirot.

" Well, Poirot," he said. " What are you thinking about? You've not opened your mouth. What do you think of the siren? Pretty hot?"

Poirot said:

" *C'est possible.*"

" Now then, you old dog. I know you Frenchmen!"

Poirot said coldly:

" I am *not* a Frenchman!"

" Well, don't tell me you haven't got an eye for a pretty girl! What do you think of her, eh?"

Hercule Poirot said:

" She is not young."

" What does that matter? A woman's as old as she looks! *Her* looks are all right."

Hercule Poirot nodded. He said:

" Yes, she is beautiful. But it is not beauty that counts in the end. It is not beauty that makes every head (except one) turn on the beach to look at her."

" It's IT, my boy," said the Major. " That's what it is—IT."

Then he said with sudden curiosity.

" What are you looking at so steadily?"

Hercule Poirot replied: " I am looking at the exception. At the one man who did not look up when she passed."

Major Barry followed his gaze to where it rested on a man of about forty, fair-haired and sun-tanned. He had a quiet pleasant face and was sitting on the beach smoking a pipe and reading *The Times*.

" Oh, *that*!" said Major Barry. " That's the husband, my boy. That's Marshall."

Hercule Poirot said:

" Yes, I know."

Major Barry chuckled. He himself was a bachelor. He was accustomed to think of The Husband in three lights only— as " the Obstacle," " the Inconvenience " or " the Safeguard."

He said:

" Seems a nice fellow. Quiet. Wonder if my *Times* has come?"

He got up and went up towards the hotel.

Poirot's glance shifted slowly to the face of Stephen Lane.

Stephen Lane was watching Arlena Marshall and Patrick Redfern. He turned suddenly to Poirot. There was a stern fanatical light in his eyes.

He said:

" That woman is evil through and through. Do you doubt it?"

Poirot said slowly:

" It is difficult to be sure."

Stephen Lane said:

" But, man alive, don't you feel it in the air? All round you? The presence of Evil."

Slowly, Hercule Poirot nodded his head.

Chapter Two

1

WHEN Rosamund Darnley came and sat down by him, Hercule Poirot made no attempt to disguise his pleasure.

As he has since admitted, he admired Rosamund Darnley as much as any woman he had ever met. He liked her distinction, the graceful lines of her figure, the alert proud carriage of her head. He liked the neat sleek waves of her dark hair and the ironic quality of her smile.

She was wearing a dress of some navy blue material with touches of white. It looked very simple owing to the expensive severity of its line. Rosamund Darnley as Rose Mond Ltd. was one of London's best-known dressmakers.

She said:

"I don't think I like this place. I'm wondering why I came here!"

"You have been here before, have you not?"

"Yes, two years ago, at Easter. There weren't so many people then."

Hercule Poirot looked at her. He said gently:

"Something has occurred to worry you. That is right, is it not?"

She nodded. Her foot swung to and fro. She stared down at it. She said:

"I've met a ghost. That's what it is."

"A ghost. Mademoiselle?"

"Yes"

"The ghost of what? Or of whom?"

"Oh, the ghost of myself."

Poirot asked gently:

"Was it a painful ghost?"

"Unexpectedly painful. It took me back, you know. . . ."

She paused, musing. Then she said:

"Imagine my childhood. No, you can't! You're not English!"

Poirot asked:

"Was it a very English childhood?"

"Oh, incredibly so! The country—a big shabby house—horses, dogs—walks in the rain—wood fires—apples in the orchard—lack of money—old tweeds—evening dresses that went on from year to year—a neglected garden—with Michaelmas daisies coming out like great banners in the autumn. . . ."

Poirot asked gently:

"And you want to go back?"

Rosamund Darnley shook her head. She said:

"One can't go back, can one? That—never. But I'd like to have gone on—a different way."

Poirot said:

"I wonder."

Rosamund Darnley laughed.

"So do I, really!"

Poirot said:

"When I was young (and that, Mademoiselle, is indeed a long time ago) there was a game entitled, '*If not yourself, who would you be?*' One wrote the answer in young ladies' albums. They had gold edges and were bound in blue leather. The answer? Mademoiselle, is not really very easy to find."

Rosamund said:

"No—I suppose not. It would be a big risk. One wouldn't like to take on being Mussolini or Princess Elizabeth. As for one's friends, one knows too much about them. I remember once meeting a charming husband and wife. They were so courteous and delightful to one another and seemed on such good terms after years of marriage that I envied the woman. I'd have changed places with her willingly. Somebody told me afterwards that in private they'd never spoken to each other for eleven years!"

She laughed.

"That shows, doesn't it, that you never know?"

After a moment or two Poirot said:

"Many people, Mademoiselle, must envy you."

Rosamund Darnley said coolly:

"Oh, yes. Naturally."

She thought about it, her lips curved upward in their ironic smile.

"Yes, I'm really the perfect type of the successful woman! I enjoy the artistic satisfaction of the successful creative artist (I really do like designing clothes) and the financial satisfaction of the successful business woman. I'm very well off, I've a good figure, a passable face, and a not too malicious tongue."

She paused. Her smile widened.

"Of course—I haven't got a husband! I've failed there, haven't I, M. Poirot?"

Poirot said gallantly:

"Mademoiselle, if you are not married, it is because none of my sex have been sufficiently eloquent. It is from choice, not necessity, that you remain single."

Rosamund Darnley said:

"And yet, like all men, I'm sure you believe in your heart that no woman is content unless she is married and has children."

Poirot shrugged his shoulders.

"To marry and have children, that is the common lot of women. Only one woman in a hundred—more, in a thousand, can make for herself a name and a position as you have done."

Rosamund grinned at him.

"And yet, all the same, I'm nothing but a wretched old maid! That's what I feel to-day, at anyrate. I'd be happier with twopence a year and a big silent brute of a husband and a brood of brats running after me. That's true, isn't it?"

Poirot shrugged his shoulders.

"Since you say so, then, yes, Mademoiselle."

Rosamund laughed, her equilibrium suddenly restored. She took out a cigarette and lit it.

She said:

"You certainly know how to deal with women, M. Poirot. I now feel like taking the opposite point of view and arguing with you in favour of careers for women. Of course I'm damned well off as I am—and I know it!"

"Then everything in the garden—or shall we say at the seaside?—is lovely, Mademoiselle."

"Quite right."

Poirot, in his turn, extracted his cigarette case and lit one of those tiny cigarettes which it was his affectation to smoke. Regarding the ascending haze with a quizzical eye, he murmured:

"So Mr.—no, Captain Marshall is an old friend of yours, Mademoiselle?"

Rosamund sat up. She said:

"Now how do you know that? Oh, I suppose Ken told you."

Poirot shook his head.

"Nobody has told me anything. After all, Mademoiselle, I am a detective. It was the obvious conclusion to draw."

Rosamund Darnley said: "I don't see it."

"But consider!" The little man's hands were eloquent. "You have been here a week. You are lively, gay, without a care. To-day, suddenly, you speak of ghosts, of old times. What has happened? For several days there have been no new arrivals until last night when Captain Marshall and his wife and daughter arrive. To-day the change! It is obvious!"

Rosamund Darnley said:

"Well, it's true enough. Kenneth Marshall and I were more or less children together. The Marshalls lived next door to us. Ken was always nice to me—although condescending, of course, since he was four years older. I've not seen anything of him for a long time. It must be—fifteen years at least."

Poirot said thoughtfully:

"A long time."

Rosamund nodded.

There was a pause and then Hercule Poirot said:

"He is sympathetic, yes?"

Rosamund said warmly:

"Ken's a dear. One of the best. Frightfully quiet and reserved. I'd say his only fault is a *penchant* for making unfortunate marriages."

Poirot said in a tone of great understanding: "Ah——"

Rosamund Darnley went on.

"Kenneth's a fool—an utter fool where women are concerned! Do you remember the Martingdale case?"

Poirot frowned.

"Martingdale? Martingdale? Arsenic, was it not?"

"Yes. Seventeen or eighteen years ago. The woman was tried for the murder of her husband."

"And he was proved to have been an arsenic eater and she was acquitted?"

"That's right. Well, after her acquittal, Ken married her. That's the sort of damn silly thing he does."

Hercule Poirot murmured:

"But if she was innocent?"

Rosamund Darnley said impatiently:

"Oh, I dare say she *was* innocent. Nobody really knows! But there are plenty of women to marry in the world without going out of your way to marry one who's stood her trial for murder."

Poirot said nothing. Perhaps he knew that if he kept silence Rosamund Darnley would go on. She did so.

"He was very young, of course, only just twenty-one. He was crazy about her. She died when Linda was born—a year after their marriage. I believe Ken was terribly cut up by her death. Afterwards he racketed around a lot—trying to forget, I suppose."

She paused.

"And then came this business of Arlena Stuart. She was in Revue at the time. There was the Codrington divorce case. Lady Codrington divorced Codrington, citing Arlena Stuart. They say Lord Codrington was absolutely infatuated with her. It was understood they were to be married as soon as the decree was made absolute. Actually, when it came to it, he didn't marry her. Turned her down flat. I believe she actually sued him for breach of promise. Anyway, the thing made a big stir at the time. The next thing that happens is that Ken goes and marries her. The fool—the complete fool!"

Hercule Poirot murmured:

"A man might, be excused such a folly—she is beautiful, Mademoiselle."

"Yes, there's no doubt of that. There was another scandal about three years ago. Old Sir Roger Erskine left her every penny of his money. I should have thought that would have opened Ken's eyes if anything would."

"And did it not?"

Rosamund Darnley shrugged her shoulders.

"I tell you I've seen nothing of him for years. People say, though, that he took it with absolute equanimity. Why, I should like to know? Has he got an absolutely blind belief in her?"

"There might be other reasons."

"Yes. Pride! Keeping a stiff upper lip! I don't know what he really feels about her. Nobody does."

"And she? What does she feel about him?"

Rosamund stared at him.

She said:

"She? She's the world's first gold-digger. And a man-eater

as well! If anything personable in trousers comes within a hundred yards of her, it's fresh sport for Arlena! She's that kind."

Poirot nodded his head slowly in complete agreement.

" Yes," he said. " That is true what you say. . . . Her eyes look for one thing only—men."

Rosamund said:

" She's got her eye on Patrick Redfern now. He's a good-looking man—and rather the simple kind—you know, fond of his wife, and not a philanderer. That's the kind that's meat and drink to Arlena. I like little Mrs. Redfern—she's nice-looking in her fair washed-out way—but I don't think she'll stand a dog's chance against that man-eating tiger, Arlena."

Poirot said:

" No, it is as you say."

He looked distressed.

Rosamund said:

" Christine Redfern was a school teacher, I believe. She's the kind that thinks that mind has a pull over matter. She's got a rude shock coming to her."

Poirot shook his head vexedly.

Rosamund got up. She said:

" It's a shame, you know." She added vaguely: " Somebody ought to do something about it."

2

Linda Marshall was examining her face dispassionately in her bedroom mirror. She disliked her face very much. At this minute it seemed to her to be mostly bones and freckles. She noted with distaste her heavy bush of soft brown hair (mouse, she called it in her own mind), her greenish-grey eyes, her high cheek-bones and the long aggressive line of the chin. Her mouth and teeth weren't perhaps quite so bad—but what were teeth after all? And was that a spot coming on the side of her nose?

She decided with relief that it wasn't a spot. She thought to herself:

" It's awful to be sixteen—simply *awful*."

One didn't, somehow, know where one was. Linda was

as awkward as a young colt and as prickly as a hedgehog.
She was conscious the whole time of her ungainliness and
of the fact that she was neither one thing nor the other. It
hadn't been so bad at school. But now she had left school. Nobody seemed to know quite what she was going to do next.
Her father talked vaguely of sending her to Paris next winter.
Linda didn't want to go to Paris—but then she didn't want
to be at home either. She'd never realised properly, somehow, until now, how very much she disliked Arlena.

Linda's young face grew tense, her green eyes hardened.
Arlena. . . .

She thought to herself:

" She's a beast—a *beast*. . . ."

Stepmothers! It was rotten to have a stepmother, everybody said so. And it was true! Not that Arlena was unkind
to her. Most of the time she hardly noticed the girl. But when
she did, there was a contemptuous amusement in her glance,
in her words. The finished grace and poise of Arlena's
movements emphasised Linda's own adolescent clumsiness.
With Arlena about, one felt, shamingly, just how immature
and crude one was.

But it wasn't that only. No, it wasn't only that.

Linda groped haltingly in the recesses of her mind. She
wasn't very good at sorting out her emotions and labelling
them. It was something that Arlena *did* to people—to the
house——

" She's bad," thought Linda with decision. " She's quite,
quite bad."

But you couldn't even leave it at that. You couldn't just
elevate your nose with a sniff of moral superiority and dismiss
her from your mind.

It was something she did to people. Father, now, father
was quite different. . . .

She puzzled over it. Father coming down to take her out
from school. Father taking her once for a cruise. And Father
at home—with Arlena there. All—all sort of bottled up
and not—and not *there*.

Linda thought:

" And it'll go on like this. Day after day—month after
month. I can't bear it."

Life stretched before her—endless—in a series of days
darkened and poisoned by Arlena's presence. She was

childish enough still to have little sense of proportion. A year, to Linda, seemed like an eternity.

A big dark burning wave of hatred against Arlena surged up in her mind. She thought:

" I'd like to kill her. Oh! I wish she'd die. . . ."

She looked out above the mirror on to the sea below.

This place was really rather fun. Or it could be fun. All those beaches and coves and queer little paths. Lots to explore. And places where one could go off by oneself and muck about. There were caves, too, so the Cowan boys had told her.

Linda thought:

" If only Arlena would go away, I could enjoy myself."

Her mind went back to the evening of their arrival. It had been exciting coming from the mainland. The tide had been up over the causeway. They had come in a boat. The hotel had looked exciting, unusual. And then on the terrace a tall dark woman had jumped up and said:

" Why, Kenneth ! "

And her father, looking frightfully surprised, had exclaimed:

" Rosamund ! "

Linda considered Rosamund Darnley severely and critically in the manner of youth.

She decided that she approved of Rosamund. Rosamund, she thought, was sensible. And her hair grew nicely—as though it fitted her—most people's hair didn't fit them. And her clothes were nice. And she had a kind of funny amused face—as though it were amused at herself, not at you. Rosamund had been nice to her, Linda. She hadn't been gushing or *said* things. (Under the term of " saying things " Linda grouped a mass of miscellaneous dislikes.) And Rosamund hadn't looked as though she thought Linda a fool. In fact she'd treated Linda as though she was a real human being. Linda so seldom felt like a real human being that she was deeply grateful when any one appeared to consider her one.

Father, too, had seemed pleased to see Miss Darnley.

Funny—he'd looked quite different, all of a sudden. He'd looked—he'd looked—Linda puzzled it out—why, *young*, that was it! He'd laughed—a queer boyish laugh. Now Linda came to think of it, she'd very seldom heard him laugh.

She felt puzzled. It was as though she'd got a glimpse of quite a different person. She thought:

"I wonder what Father was like when he was my age. . . ."

But that was too difficult. She gave it up.

An idea flashed across her mind.

What fun it would have been if they'd come here and found Miss Darnley here—just she and Father.

A vista opened out just for a minute. Father, boyish and laughing, Miss Darnley, herself—and all the fun one could have on the island—bathing—caves——

The blackness shut down again.

Arlena. One couldn't enjoy oneself with Arlena about. Why not? Well, she, Linda, couldn't, anyway. You couldn't be happy when there was a person there you—hated. Yes, hated. She hated Arlena.

Very slowly again that black burning wave of hatred rose up again.

Linda's face went very white. Her lips parted a little. The pupils of her eyes contracted. And her fingers stiffened and clenched themselves. . . .

3

Kenneth Marshall tapped on his wife's door. When her voice answered, he opened the door and went in.

Arlena was just putting the finishing touches to her toilet. She was dressed in glittering green and looked a little like a mermaid. She was standing in front of the glass applying mascara to her eyelashes. She said:

"Oh, it's you, Ken."

"Yes. I wondered if you were ready."

"Just a minute."

Kenneth Marshall strolled to the window. He looked out on the sea. His face, as usual, displayed no emotion of any kind. It was pleasant and ordinary.

Turning round, he said:

"Arlena?"

"Yes?"

"You've met Redfern before, I gather?"

Arlena said easily:

"Oh yes, darling. At a cocktail party somewhere. I thought he was rather a pet."

"So I gather. Did you know that he and his wife were coming down here?"

Arlena opened her eyes very wide.

"Oh no, darling. It was the *greatest* surprise!"

Kenneth Marshall said quietly:

"I thought, perhaps, that that was what put the idea of this place into your head. You were very keen we should come here."

Arlena put down the mascara. She turned towards him. She smiled—a soft seductive smile. She said:

"Somebody told me about this place. I think it was the Rylands. They said it was simply too marvellous—so unspoilt! Don't you like it?"

Kenneth Marshall said:

"I'm not sure."

"Oh, darling, but you adore bathing and lazing about. I'm sure you'll simply adore it here."

"I can see that you mean to enjoy yourself."

Her eyes widened a little. She looked at him uncertainly.

Kenneth Marshall said:

"I suppose the truth of it is that you told young Redfern that you were coming here?"

Arlena said:

"Kenneth darling, you're not going to be horrid, are you?"

Kenneth Marshall said:

"Look here, Arlena. I know what you're like. They're rather a nice young couple. That boy's fond of his wife, really. Must you upset the whole blinking show?"

Arlena said:

"It's so unfair blaming *me*. *I* haven't done anything—anything at all. I can't help it if——"

He prompted her.

"If what?"

Her eyelids fluttered.

"Well. of course, I know people do go crazy about me. But it's not my doing. They just get like that."

"So you do admit that young Redfern is crazy about you?"

Arlena murmured:

"It's really rather stupid of him."

She moved a step towards her husband.

"But you know, don't you, Ken, that I don't really care for any one but you?"

She looked up at him through her darkened lashes.

It was a marvellous look—a look that few men could have resisted.

Kenneth Marshall looked down at her gravely. His face was composed. His voice quiet. He said:

"I think I know you pretty well, Arlena. . . ."

4

When you came out of the hotel on the south side the terraces and the bathing beach were immediately below you. There was also a path that led off round the cliff on the south-west side of the island. A little way along it, a few steps led down to a series of recesses cut into the cliff and labelled on the hotel map of the island as Sunny Ledge. Here cut out of the cliff were niches with seats in them.

To one of these, immediately after dinner, came Patrick Redfern and his wife. It was a lovely clear night with a bright moon.

The Redferns sat down. For a while they were silent.

At last Patrick Redfern said:

"It's a glorious evening, isn't it, Christine?"

"Yes."

Something in her voice may have made him uneasy. He sat without looking at her.

Christine Redfern asked in her quiet voice:

"Did you know that woman was going to be here?"

He turned sharply. He said:

"I don't know what you mean."

"I think you do."

"Look here, Christine. I don't know what has come over you——"

She interrupted. Her voice held feeling now. It trembled.

"Over *me*? It's what has come over *you*!"

"Nothing's come over me."

"Oh! Patrick! it *has*! You insisted so on coming here. You were quite vehement. I wanted to go to Tintagel again where—where we had our honeymoon. You were bent on coming here."

" Well, why not? It's a fascinating spot."

" Perhaps. But you wanted to come here because *she* was going to be here."

" She? Who is she?"

" Mrs. Marshall. You—you're infatuated with her."

" For God's sake, Christine, don't make a fool of yourself. It's not like you to be jealous."

His bluster was a little uncertain. He exaggerated it.
She said:

" We've been so happy."

" Happy? Of course we've been happy! We *are* happy. But we shan't go on being happy if I can't even speak to another woman without you kicking up a row."

" It's not like that."

" Yes, it is. In marriage one has got to have—well—friendships with other people. This suspicious attitude is all wrong. I—I can't speak to a pretty woman without your jumping to the conclusion that I'm in love with her——"

He stopped. He shrugged his shoulders.

Christine Redfern said:

" You *are* in love with her. . . ."

" Oh, don't be a fool, Christine! I've—I've barely spoken to her."

" That's not true."

" Don't for goodness' sake get into the habit of being jealous of every pretty woman we come across."

Christine Redfern said:

" She's not just any pretty woman! She's—she's *different*! She's a bad lot! Yes, she is. She'll do you harm, Patrick, please, *give it up*. Let's go away from here."

Patrick Redfern stuck out his chin mutinously. He looked, somehow, very young as he said defiantly:

" Don't be ridiculous, Christine. And—and don't let's quarrel about it."

" I don't want to quarrel."

" Then behave like a reasonable human being. Come on, let's go back to the hotel."

He got up. There was a pause, then Christine Redfern got up too.

She said:

" Very well. . . ."

In the recess adjoining, on the seat there, Hercule Poirot sat and shook his head sorrowfully.

Some people might have scrupulously removed themselves from earshot of a private conversation. But not Hercule Poirot. He had no scruples of that kind.

" Besides," as he explained to his friend Hastings at a later date, " it was a question of murder."

Hastings said, staring:

" But the murder hadn't happened, then."

Hercule Poirot sighed. He said:

" But already, *mon cher*, it was very clearly indicated."

" Then why didn't you stop it?"

And Hercule Poirot, with a sigh, said as he had said once before in Egypt, that if a person is determined to commit murder it is not easy to prevent them. He does not blame himself for what happened. It was, according to him, inevitable

Chapter Three

1

ROSAMUND DARNLEY and Kenneth Marshall sat on the short springy turf of the cliff overlooking Gull Cove. This was on the east side of the island. People came here in the morning sometimes to bathe when they wanted to be peaceful.

Rosamund said:

" It's nice to get away from people."

Marshall murmured inaudibly:

" M—m, yes."

He rolled over, sniffing at the short turf.

" Smells good. Remember the downs at Shipley?"

" Rather."

" Pretty good, those days."

" Yes."

" You've not changed much, Rosamund."

" Yes, I have. I've changed enormously."

" You've been very successful and you're rich and all that, but you're the same old Rosamund."

Rosamund murmured:

"I wish I were."

"What's that?"

"Nothing. It's a pity, isn't it, Kenneth, that we can't keep the nice natures and high ideals that we had when we were young?"

"I don't know that your nature was ever particularly nice, my child. You used to get into the most frightful rages. You half-choked me once when you flew at me in a temper."

Rosamund laughed. She said:

"Do you remember the day that we took Toby down to get water rats?"

They spent some minutes in recalling old adventures.

Then there came a pause.

Rosamund's fingers played with the clasp of her bag. She said at last:

"Kenneth?"

"Um." His reply was indistinct. He was still lying on his face on the turf.

"If I say something to you that is probably outrageously impertinent will you never speak to me again?"

He rolled over and sat up.

"I don't think," he said seriously, "that I would ever regard anything you said as impertinent. You see, you *belong*."

She nodded in acceptance of all that last phrase meant. She concealed only the pleasure it gave her.

"Kenneth, why don't you get a divorce from your wife?"

His face altered. It hardened—the happy expression died out of it. He took a pipe from his pocket and began filling it.

Rosamund said:

"I'm sorry if I've offended you."

He said quietly:

"You haven't offended me."

"Well, then, why don't you?"

"You don't understand, my dear girl."

"Are you—so frightfully fond of her?"

"It's not just a question of that. You see. I married her."

"I know. But she's—pretty notorious."

He considered that for a moment, ramming in the tobacco carefully.

"Is she? I suppose she is."

"You *could* divorce her, Ken."

" My dear girl, you've got no business to say a thing like that. Just because men lose their heads about her a bit isn't to say that she loses hers "

Rosamund bit off a rejoinder. Then she said:

" You could fix it so that she divorced you—if you prefer it that way."

" I dare say I could."

" You ought to, Ken. Really, I mean it. There's the child."

" Linda?"

" Yes, Linda."

" What's Linda to do with it?"

" Arlena's not good for Linda. She isn't really. Linda I think, *feels* things a good deal."

Kenneth Marshall applied a match to his pipe. Between puffs he said:

" Yes—there's something in that. I suppose Arlena and Linda aren't very good for each other. Not the right thing for a girl perhaps. It's a bit worrying."

Rosamund said:

" I like Linda—very much. There's something—fine about her."

Kenneth said:

" She's like her mother. She takes things hard like Ruth did."

Rosamund said:

" Then don't you think—really—that you ought to get rid of Arlena?"

" Fix up a divorce?"

" Yes. People are doing that all the time."

Kenneth Marshall said with sudden vehemence:

" Yes, and that's just what I hate."

" Hate?" She was startled.

" Yes. Sort of attitude to life there is nowadays. If you take on a thing and don't like it, then you get yourself out of it as quick as possible! Dash it all, there's got to be such a thing as good faith. If you marry a woman and engage yourself to look after her, well, it's up to you to do it. It's your show. You've taken it on. I'm sick of quick marriage and easy divorce Arlena's my wife, that's all there is to it."

Rosamund leaned forward. She said in a low voice:

" So it's like that with you? ' Till death do us part'?"

Kenneth Marshall nodded his head.

He said:
"That's just it."
Rosamund said:
"I see."

2

Mr. Horace Blatt, returning to Leathercombe Bay down a narrow twisting lane, nearly ran down Mrs. Redfern at a corner.

As she flattened herself into the hedge, Mr. Blatt brought his Sunbeam to a halt by applying the brakes vigorously.

"Hullo-ullo-ullo," said Mr. Blatt cheerfully.

He was a large man with a red face and a fringe of reddish hair round a shining bald spot.

It was Mr. Blatt's apparent ambition to be the life and soul of any place he happened to be in. The Jolly Roger Hotel, in his opinion, given somewhat loudly, needed brightening up. He was puzzled at the way people seemed to melt and disappear when he himself arrived on the scene.

"Nearly made you into strawberry jam, didn't I?" said Mr. Blatt gaily.

Christine Redfern said:
"Yes, you did."

"Jump in," said Mr. Blatt.

"Oh, thanks—I think I'll walk."

"Nonsense," said Mr. Blatt. "What's a car for?"

Yielding to necessity Christine Redfern got in.

Mr. Blatt restarted the engine which had stopped owing to the suddenness with which he had previously pulled up.

Mr. Blatt inquired:

"And what are you doing walking about all alone? That's all wrong, a nice-looking girl like you."

Christine said hurriedly:

"Oh! I like being alone."

Mr. Blatt gave her a terrific dig with his elbow, nearly sending the car into the hedge at the same time.

"Girls always say that," he said. "They don't mean it. You know, that place, the Jolly Roger, wants a bit of livening up. Nothing jolly about it. No *life* in it. Of course there's a good amount of duds staying there. A lot of kids, to begin

with and a lot of old fogeys too. There's that old Angl-
Indian bore and that athletic parson and those yapping
Americans and that foreigner with the moustache—makes
me laugh that moustache of his! I should say he's a hair-
dresser, something of that sort."

Christine shook her head.

" Oh no, he's a detective."

Mr. Blatt nearly let the car go into the hedge again.

" A detective? D'you mean he's in *disguise*?"

Christine smiled faintly.

She said:

" Oh no, he really *is* like that. He's Hercule Poirot. You
must have heard of him."

Mr. Blatt said:

" Didn't catch his name properly. Oh yes, I've *heard* of
him. But I thought he was dead. . . . Dash it, he *ought* to
be dead. What's he after down here?"

" He's not after anything—he's just on a holiday."

" Well, I suppose that might be so," Mr. Blatt seemed
doubtful about it. " Looks a bit of a bounder, doesn't he?"

" Well," said Christine and hesitated. " Perhaps a little
peculiar."

" What I say is," said Mr. Blatt, " what's wrong with
Scotland Yard? Buy British every time for me."

He reached the bottom of the hill and with a triumphant
fanfare of the horn ran the car into the Jolly Roger's garage
which was situated, for tidal reasons, on the mainland
opposite the hotel.

3

Linda Marshall was in the small shop which catered for the
wants of visitors to Leathercombe Bay. One side of it
was devoted to shelves on which were books which could be
borrowed for the sum of twopence. The newest of them was
ten years old, some were twenty years old and others older
still.

Linda took first one and then another doubtfully from the
shelf and glanced into it. She decided that she couldn't
possibly read *The Four Feathers* or *Vice Versa*. She took
out a small squat volume in brown calf.

The time passed. . . .

With a start Linda shoved the book back in the shelf as Christine Redfern's voice said:

" What are you reading, Linda?"

Linda said hurriedly:

" Nothing. I'm looking for a book."

She pulled out *The Marriage of William Ashe* at random and advanced to the counter fumbling for twopence.

Christine said:

" Mr Blatt just drove me home—after nearly running over me first. I really felt I couldn't walk all across the causeway with him. so I said I had to buy some things."

Linda said:

" He's awful, isn't he? Always saying how rich he is and making the most terrible jokes."

Christine said:

" Poor man. One really feels rather sorry for him."

Linda didn't agree. She didn't see anything to be sorry for in Mr Blatt. She was young and ruthless.

She walked with Christine Redfern out of the shop and down towards the causeway.

She was busy with her own thoughts. She liked Christine Redfern. She and Rosamund Darnley were the only bearable people on the island in Linda's opinion. Neither of them talked much to her for one thing. Now, as they walked, Christine didn't say anything. That, Linda thought, was sensible. If you hadn't anything worth saying why go chattering all the time?

She lost herself in her own perplexities.

She said suddenly:

" Mrs. Redfern, have you ever felt that everything's so awful—so terrible—that you'll—oh, *burst* . . .?"

The words were almost comic, but Linda's face, drawn and anxious, was not. Christine Redfern, looking at her at first vaguely, with scarcely comprehending eyes, certainly saw nothing to laugh at. . . .

She caught her breath sharply.

She said:

" Yes—yes—I have felt—just that. . . ."

4

Mr. Blatt said:

"So you're the famous sleuth, eh?"

They were in the cocktail bar, a favourite haunt of Mr. Blatt's.

Hercule Poirot acknowledged the remark with his usual lack of modesty.

Mr. Blatt went on.

"And what are you doing down here—on a job?"

"No, no. I repose myself. I take the holiday."

Mr. Blatt winked.

"You'd say that anyway, wouldn't you?"

Poirot replied:

"Not necessarily."

Horace Blatt said:

"Oh! come now. As a matter of fact you'd be safe enough with *me*. *I* don't repeat all I hear! Learnt to keep my mouth shut years ago. Shouldn't have got on the way I have if I hadn't known how to do that. But you know what most people are—yap, yap, yap about everything they hear! Now you can't afford that in your trade! That's why you've got to keep it up that you're here holiday-making and nothing else."

Poirot asked:

"And why should you suppose the contrary?"

Mr. Blatt closed one eye.

He said:

"I'm a man of the world. I know the cut of a fellow's jib. A man like you would be at Deauville or Le Touquet or down at Juan les Pins. That's your—what's the phrase?—spiritual home."

Poirot sighed. He looked out of the window. Rain was falling and mist encircled the island. He said:

"It is possible that you are right! There, at least, in wet weather there are the distractions."

"Good old Casino!" said Mr. Blatt. "You know, I've had to work pretty hard most of my life. No time for holidays or kickshaws. I meant to make good and I have made good. Now I can do what I please. My money's as good

as any man's. I've seen a bit of life in the last few years,
I can tell you."

Poirot murmured:

"Ah, yes?"

"Don't know why I came to this place," Mr. Blatt
continued.

Poirot observed:

"I, too, wondered?"

"Eh, what's that?"

Poirot waved an eloquent hand.

"I, too, am not without observation. I should have expected
you most certainly to choose Deauville or Biarritz."

"Instead of which, we're both here, eh?"

Mr. Blatt gave a hoarse chuckle.

"Don't really know why I came here," he mused. "I think,
you know, it sounded *romantic*. Jolly Roger Hotel,
Smugglers' Island. That kind of address tickles you up, you
know. Makes you think of when you were a boy. Pirates,
smuggling, all that."

He laughed rather self-consciously.

"I used to sail quite a bit as a boy. Not this part of the
world. Off the East coast. Funny how a taste for that sort
of thing never quite leaves you. I could have a tip-top yacht
if I liked, but somehow I don't really fancy it. I like mucking
about in that little yawl of mine. Redfern's keen on sailing,
too. He's been out with me once or twice. Can't get hold
of him now—always hanging round that red-haired wife of
Marshall's."

He paused, then lowering his voice, he went on:

"Mostly a dried up lot of sticks in this hotel! Mrs.
Marshall's about the only lively spot! I should think
Marshall's got his hands full looking after her. All sorts of
stories about her in her stage days—*and* after! Men go crazy
about her. You'll see, there'll be a spot of trouble one of
these days."

Poirot asked: "What kind of trouble?"

Horace Blatt replied:

"That depends. I'd say, looking at Marshall, that he's a
man with a funny kind of temper. As a matter of fact, I
know he is. Heard something about him. I've met that quiet
sort. Never know where you are with that kind. Redfern had
better look out——"

He broke off, as the subject of his words came into the bar. He went on speaking loudly and self-consciously.

" And, as I say, sailing round this coast is good fun. Hullo, Redfern, have one with me? What'll you have? Dry Martini? Right. What about you, M. Poirot?"

Poirot shook his head.

Patrick Redfern sat down and said :

" Sailing? It's the best fun in the world. Wish I could do more of it. Used to spend most of my time as a boy in a sailing dinghy round this coast."

Poirot said :

" Then you know this part of the world well?"

" Rather! I knew this place before there was a hotel on it. There were just a few fishermen's cottages at Leathercombe Bay and a tumbledown old house, all shut up, on the island."

" There was a house here?"

" Oh, yes, but it hadn't been lived in for years. Was practically falling down. There used to be all sorts of stories of secret passages from the house to Pixy's Cave. We were always looking for that secret passage, I remember."

Horace Blatt spilt his drink. He cursed, mopped himself and asked :

" What is this Pixy's Cave?"

Patrick said :

" Oh, don't you know it? It's on Pixy Cove. You can't find the entrance to it easily. It's among a lot of piled up boulders at one end. Just a long thin crack. You can just squeeze through it. Inside it widens out into quite a big cave. You can imagine what fun it was to a boy! An old fisherman showed it to me. Nowadays, even the fishermen don't know about it. I asked one the other day why the place was called Pixy Cove and he couldn't tell me."

Hercule Poirot said :

" But I still do not understand. What is this pixy?"

Patrick Redfern said :

" Oh! that's typically Devonshire. There's the pixy's cave at Sheepstor on the Moor. You're supposed to leave a pin, you know, as a present for the pixy. A pixy is a kind of moor spirit."

Hercule Poirot said :

" Ah! but it is interesting, that."

Patrick Redfern went on.

"There's a lot of pixy lore on Dartmoor still. There are tors that are said to be pixy ridden, and I expect that farmers coming home after a thick night still complain of being pixy led."

Horace Blatt said:

"You mean when they've had a couple?"

Patrick Redfern said with a smile:

"That's certainly the commonsense explanation!"

Blatt looked at his watch. He said:

"I'm going in to dinner. On the whole, Redfern, pirates are my favourites, not pixies."

Patrick Redfern said with a laugh as the other went out:

"Faith, I'd like to see the old boy pixy led himself!"

Poirot observed meditatively:

"For a hard-bitten business man, M. Blatt seems to have a very romantic imagination."

Patrick Redfern said:

"That's because he's only half educated. Or so my wife says. Look at what he reads! Nothing but thrillers or Wild West stories."

Poirot said:

"You mean that he has still the mentality of a boy?"

"Well, don't you think so, sir?"

"Me, I have not seen very much of him."

"I haven't either. I've been out sailing with him once or twice—but he doesn't really like having any one with him. He prefers to be on his own."

Hercule Poirot said:

"That is indeed curious. It is singularly unlike his practice on land."

Redfern laughed. He said:

"I know. We all have a bit of trouble keeping out of his way. He'd like to turn this place into a cross between Margate and Le Touquet."

Poirot said nothing for a minute or two. He was studying the laughing face of his companion very attentively. He said suddenly and unexpectedly:

"I think, M. Redfern, that you enjoy living."

Patrick stared at him, surprised.

"Indeed I do. Why not?"

"Why not indeed," agreed Poirot. "I make you my felicitation on the fact."

Smiling a little, Patrick Redfern said:

"Thank you, sir."

"That is why, as an older man, a very much older man, I venture to offer you a piece of advice."

"Yes, sir?"

"A very wise friend of mine in the Police Force said to me years ago: 'Hercule, my friend, if you would know tranquillity, avoid women.'"

Patrick Redfern said:

"I'm afraid it's a bit late for that, sir. I'm married, you know."

"I do know. Your wife is a very charming, a very accomplished woman. She is, I think, very fond of you."

Patrick Redfern said sharply:

"I'm very fond of her."

"Ah," said Hercule Poirot, "I am delighted to hear it."

Patrick's brow was suddenly like thunder.

"Look here, M. Poirot, what are you getting at?"

"*Les Femmes*," Poirot leaned back and closed his eyes. "I know something of them. They are capable of complicating life unbearably. And the English, they conduct their affairs indescribably. If it was necessary for you to come here, M. Redfern, why, in the name of heaven, did you bring your wife?"

Patrick Redfern said angrily:

"I don't know what you mean."

Hercule Poirot said calmly:

"You know perfectly. I am not so foolish as to argue with an infatuated man. I utter only the word of caution."

"You've been listening to these damned scandal-mongers. Mrs. Gardener, the Brewster woman—nothing to do but to clack their tongues all day. Just because a woman's good-looking—they're down on her like a sack of coals."

Hercule Poirot got up. He murmured:

"Are you really as young as all that?"

Shaking his head, he left the bar. Patrick Redfern stared angrily after him.

5

Hercule Poirot paused in the hall on his way from the dining-room. The doors were open—a breath of soft night air came in.

The rain had stopped and the mist had dispersed. It was a fine night again.

Hercule Poirot found Mrs. Redfern in her favourite seat on the cliff ledge. He stopped by her and said:

" This seat is damp. You should not sit here. You will catch the chill."

" No, I shan't. And what does it matter anyway."

" Tscha, tscha, you are not a child! You are an educated woman. You must look at things sensibly."

She said coldly:

" I can assure you I never take cold."

Poirot said:

" It has been a wet day. The wind blew, the rain came down, and the mist was everywhere so that one could not see through it. *Eh bien*, what is it like now? The mists have rolled away, the sky is clear and up above the stars shine. That is like life, Madame."

Christine said in a low fierce voice:

" Do you know what I am most sick of in this place?"

" What, Madame?"

" Pity."

She brought the word out like the flick of a whip.

She went on:

" Do you think I don't know? That I can't see? All the time people are saying: ' Poor Mrs. Redfern—that poor little woman.' And anyway I'm not little, I'm tall. They say little because they are sorry for me. And I can't bear it!"

Cautiously, Hercule Poirot spread his handkerchief on the seat and sat down. He said thoughtfully:

" There is something in that."

" That woman——" said Christine and stopped.

Poirot said gravely:

" Will you allow me to tell you something, Madame? Something that is as true as the stars above us? The Arlena

Stuarts—or Arlena Marshalls—of this world—do not count."

Christine Redfern said:

"Nonsense."

"I assure you, it is true. Their Empire is of the moment and for the moment. To count—really and truly to count—a woman must have goodness or brains."

Christine said scornfully:

"Do you think men care for goodness or brains?"

Poirot said gravely:

"Fundamentally, yes."

Christine laughed shortly.

"I don't agree with you."

Poirot said:

"Your husband loves you, Madame. I know it."

"You can't know it."

"Yes, yes. I know it. I have seen him looking at you."

Suddenly she broke down. She wept stormily and bitterly against Poirot's accommodating shoulder.

She said:

"I can't bear it. . . . I can't bear it. . . ."

Poirot patted her arm. He said soothingly:

"Patience—only patience."

She sat up and pressed her handkerchief to her eyes. She said in a stifled voice:

"It's all right. I'm better now. Leave me. I'd—I'd rather be alone"

He obeyed and left her sitting there while he himself followed the winding path down to the hotel.

He was nearly there when he heard the murmur of voices.

He turned a little aside from the path. There was a gap in the bushes.

He saw Arlena Marshall and Patrick Redfern beside her. He heard the man's voice, with the throb in it of emotion.

"I'm crazy about you—crazy—you've driven me mad. . . . You do care a little—you do care?"

He saw Arlena Marshall's face—it was, he thought, like a sleek happy cat—it was animal, not human. She said softly:

"Of course, Patrick darling, I adore you. You know that. . . ."

For once Hercule Poirot cut his eavesdropping short. He went back to the path and on down to the hotel.

A figure joined him suddenly. It was Captain Marshall.
Marshall said:

"Remarkable night, what? After that foul day." He
looked up at the sky. "Looks as though we should have
fine weather to-morrow."

Chapter Four

1

THE MORNING of the 25th of August dawned bright and
cloudless. It was a morning to tempt even an inveterate
sluggard to rise early.

Several people rose early that morning at the Jolly Roger.

It was eight o'clock when Linda, sitting at her dressing-table
turned a little thick calf bound volume face downwards,
sprawling it open and looked at her own face in the mirror.

Her lips were set tight together and the pupils of her
eyes contracted.

She said below her breath:
"I'll do it.   "

She slipped out of her pyjamas and into her bathing-dress.
Over it she flung on a bath-robe and laced espadrilles on her
feet.

She went out of her room and along the passage. At the end
of it a door on to the balcony led to an outside staircase
leading directly down to the rocks below the hotel. There
was a small iron ladder clamped on to the rocks leading down
into the water which was used by many of the hotel guests
for a before-breakfast dip as taking up less time than going
down to the main bathing beach.

As Linda started down from the balcony she met her father
coming up. He said:
"You're up early. Going to have a dip?"

Linda nodded.

They passed each other.

Instead of going on down the rocks, however, Linda skirted
round the hotel to the left until she came to the path down
to the causeway connecting the hotel with the mainland. The
tide was high and the causeway under water, but the boat that

took hotel guests across was tied to a little jetty. The man in charge of it was absent at the moment. Linda got in, untied it and rowed herself across.

She tied up the boat on the other side, walked up the slope, past the hotel garage and along until she reached the general shop.

The woman had just taken down the shutters and was engaged in sweeping out the floor. She looked amazed at the sight of Linda.

" Well, Miss, you *are* up early."

Linda put her hand in the pocket of her bathwrap and brought out some money. She proceeded to make her purchases.

2

Christine Redfern was standing in Linda's room when the girl returned.

" Oh, there you are," Christine exclaimed. " I thought you couldn't be really up yet."

Linda said:

" No, I've been bathing."

Noticing the parcel in her hand, Christine said with surprise:

" The post has come early to-day."

Linda flushed. With her habitual nervous clumsiness the parcel slipped from her hand. The flimsy string broke and some of the contents rolled over the floor.

Christine exclaimed:

" What have you been buying *candles* for?"

But to Linda's relief she did not wait for an answer, but went on, as she helped to pick the things up from the floor!

" I came in to ask whether you would like to come with me to Gull Cove this morning. I want to sketch there."

Linda accepted with alacrity.

In the last few days she had accompanied Christine Redfern more than once on sketching expeditions. Christine was a most indifferent artist, but it is possible that she found the excuse of painting a help to her pride since her husband now spent most of his time with Arlena Marshall.

Linda Marshall had been increasingly morose and bad tempered. She liked being with Christine who, intent on her work, spoke very little. It was, Linda felt, nearly as good as being by oneself, and in a curious way she craved for company of some kind. There was a subtle kind of sympathy between her and the elder woman, probably based on the fact of their mutual dislike of the same person.

Christine said:

"I'm playing tennis at twelve, so we'd better start fairly early. Half-past ten?"

"Right. I'll be ready. Meet you in the hall."

3

Rosamund Darnley, strolling out of the dining-room after a very late breakfast, was cannoned into by Linda as the latter came tearing down the stairs.

"Oh! sorry, Miss Darnley."

Rosamund said: "Lovely morning, isn't it? One can hardly believe it after yesterday."

"I know. I'm going with Mrs. Redfern to Gull Cove. I said I'd meet her at half-past ten. I thought I was late."

"No, it's only twenty-five past."

"Oh! good."

She was panting a little and Rosamund looked at her curiously.

"You're not feverish, are you, Linda?"

The girls' eyes were very bright and she had a vivid patch of colour in each cheek.

"Oh! *no*. I'm never feverish."

Rosamund smiled and said:

"It's such a lovely day I got up for breakfast. Usually I have it in bed. But to-day I came down and faced eggs and bacon like a man."

"I know—it's heavenly after yesterday. Gull Cove is nice in the morning. I shall put a lot of oil on and get really brown."

Rosamund said:

"Yes, Gull Cove is nice in the morning. And it's more peaceful than the beach here."

Linda said, rather shyly:

"Come too."

Rosamund shook her head.

She said:

" Not this morning. I've other fish to fry."

Christine Redfern came down the stairs.

She was wearing beach pyjamas of a loose floppy pattern with long sleeves and wide legs. They were made of some green material with a yellow design. Rosamund's tongue itched to tell her that yellow and green were the most unbecoming colours possible for her fair, slightly anæmic complexion. It always annoyed Rosamund when people had no clothes sense.

She thought: " If I dressed that girl, *I'd* soon make her husband sit up and take notice. However much of a fool Arlena is, she does know how to dress. This wretched girl looks just like a wilting lettuce."

Aloud she said:

" Have a nice time. I'm going to Sunny Ledge with a book."

4

Hercule Poirot breakfasted in his room as usual off coffee and rolls.

The beauty of the morning, however, tempted him to leave the hotel earlier than usual. It was ten o'clock, at least half an hour before his usual appearance, when he descended to the bathing beach. The beach itself was empty save for one person.

That person was Arlena Marshall.

Clad in her white bathing-dress, the green Chinese hat on her head, she was trying to launch a white wooden float. Poirot came gallantly to the rescue, completely immersing a pair of white suède shoes in doing so.

She thanked him with one of those sideways glances of hers. Just as she was pushing off, she called him.

" M. Poirot?"

Poirot leaped to the water's edge.

" Madame."

Arlena Marshall said:

" Do something for me, will you?"

" Anything."

She smiled at him. She murmured:

" Don't tell any one where I am." She made her glance

appealing. "Every one *will* follow me about so. I just want for once to be *alone*."

She paddled off vigorously.

Poirot walked up the beach. He murmured to himself:

" *Ah ça, jamais!* That, *par exemple,* I do not believe."

He doubted if Arlena Stuart, to give her her stage name, had ever wanted to be alone in her life.

Hercule Poirot, that man of the world, knew better. Arlena Marshall was doubtless keeping a rendezvous, and Poirot had a very good idea with whom.

Or thought he had, but there he found himself proved wrong.

For just as the float rounded the point of the bay and disappeared out of sight, Patrick Redfern closely followed by Kenneth Marshall, came striding down the beach from the hotel.

Marshall nodded to Poirot. " 'Morning, Poirot. Seen my wife anywhere about?"

Poirot's answer was diplomatic.

" Has Madame then risen so early?"

Marshall said:

" She's not in her room." He looked up at the sky. " Lovely day. I shall have a bathe right away. Got a lot of typing to do this morning."

Patrick Redfern, less openly, was looking up and down the beach. He sat down near Poirot and prepared to wait for the arrival of his lady.

Poirot said:

" And Madame Redfern? Has she too risen early?"

Patrick Redfern said:

" Christine? Oh, she's going off sketching. She's rather keen on art just now."

He spoke impatiently, his mind clearly elsewhere. As time passed he displayed his impatience for Arlena's arrival only too crudely. At every footstep he turned an eager head to see who it was coming down from the hotel.

Disappointment followed disappointment.

First Mr. and Mrs. Gardener complete with knitting and book and then Miss Brewster arrived.

Mrs. Gardener, industrious as ever, settled herself in her chair, and began to knit vigorously and talk at the same time.

" Well, M. Poirot. The beach seems very deserted this morning. Where *is* everybody?"

Poirot replied that the Mastermans and the Cowans, two families with young people in them, had gone off on an all-day sailing excursion.

" Why that certainly does make all the difference, not having them about laughing and calling out. And only one person bathing, Captain Marshall."

Marshall had just finished his swim. He came up the beach swinging his towel.

" Pretty good in the sea this morning," he said. " Unfortunately I've got a lot of work to do. Must go and get on with it."

" Why, if that isn't too bad, Captain Marshall. On a beautiful day like this, too. My, wasn't yesterday too terrible? I said to Mr. Gardener that if the weather was going to continue like that we'd just have to leave. It's the melancholy, you know, with the mist right up around the island. Gives you a kind of ghostly feeling, but then I've always been very susceptible to atmosphere ever since I was a child. Sometimes, you know, I'd feel I just had to scream and scream. And that, of course, was very trying to my parents. But my mother was a lovely woman and she said to my father, ' Sinclair, if the child feels like that, we must let her do it. Screaming is her way of expressing herself.' And of course, my father agreed. He was devoted to my mother and just did everything she said. They were a perfectly lovely couple, as I'm sure Mr. Gardener will agree. They were a very remarkable couple, weren't they, Odell?"

" Yes, darling," said Mr. Gardener.

" And where's your girl this morning, Captain Marshall?"

" Linda? I don't know. I expect she's mooning round the island somewhere."

" You know, Captain Marshall, that girl looks kind of peaky to me. She needs feeding up and very very sympathetic treatment."

Kenneth Marshall said curtly:

" Linda all right."

He went up to the hotel.

Patrick Redfern did not go into the water. He sat about, frankly looking up towards the hotel. He was beginning to look a shade sulky.

Miss Brewster was brisk and cheerful when she arrived.

The conversation was much as it had been on a previous morning. Gentle yapping from Mrs. Gardener and short staccato barks from Miss Brewster.

She remarked at last: "Beach seems a bit empty. Every one off on excursions?"

Mrs. Gardener said:

"I was saying to Mr. Gardener only this morning that we simply must make an excursion to Dartmoor. It's quite near and the associations are all so romantic. And I'd like to see that convict prison—Princetown, isn't it? I think we'd better fix up right away and go there to-morrow, Odell."

Mr. Gardener said:

"Yes, darling."

Hercule Poirot said to Miss Brewster.

"You are going to bathe, Mademoiselle?"

"Oh I've had my morning dip before breakfast. Somebody nearly brained me with a bottle, too. Chucked it out of one of the hotel windows."

"Now that's a very dangerous thing to do," said Mrs. Gardener. "I had a very dear friend who got concussion by a toothpaste tin falling on him in the street—thrown out of a thirty-fifth storey window it was. A most dangerous thing to do. He got very substantial damages." She began to hunt among her skeins of wool. "Why, Odell, I don't believe I've got that second shade of purple wool. It's in the second drawer of the bureau in our bedroom or it might be the third."

"Yes, darling."

Mr. Gardener rose obediently and departed on his search. Mrs. Gardener went on.

"Sometimes, you know, I do think that maybe we're going a little too far nowadays. What with all our great discoveries and all the electrical waves there must be in the atmosphere, I do think it leads to a great deal of mental unrest, and I just feel that maybe the time has come for a new message to humanity. I don't know, M. Poirot, if you've ever interested yourself in the prophecies from the Pyramids."

"I have not," said Poirot.

"Well, I do assure you that they're very, very interesting. What with Moscow being exactly a thousand miles due north of—now what was it?—would it be Nineveh?—but anyway you take a circle and it just shows the most surprising things—and one can just see that there must have been special guidance, and that those ancient Egyptians couldn't have thought of what they did all by themselves. And when you've gone into the theory of the numbers and their repetition, why it's all just so clear that I can't see how any one can doubt the truth of it for a moment."

Mrs. Gardener paused triumphantly but neither Poirot nor Miss Emily Brewster felt moved to argue the point.

Poirot studied his white suède shoes ruefully.

Emily Brewster said:

"You been paddling with your shoes on, M. Poirot?"

Poirot murmured:

"Alas! I was precipitate."

Emily Brewster lowered her voice. She said:

"Where's our vamp this morning? She's late."

Mrs. Gardener, raising her eyes from her knitting to study Patrick Redfern, murmured:

"He looks just like a thundercloud. Oh dear, I do feel the whole thing is such a pity. I wonder what Captain Marshall thinks about it all. He's such a nice quiet man— very British and unassuming. You just never know what he's thinking about things."

Patrick Redfern rose and began to pace up and down the beach.

Mrs. Gardener murmured:

"Just like a tiger."

Three pairs of eyes watched his pacing. Their scrutiny seemed to make Patrick Redfern uncomfortable. He looked more than sulky now. He looked in a flaming temper.

In the stillness a faint chime from the mainland came to their ears.

Emily Brewster murmured:

"Wind's from the east again. That's a good sign when you can hear the church clock strike."

Nobody said any more until Mr. Gardener returned with a skein of brilliant magenta wool.

"Why, Odell, what a long time you have been?"

"Sorry darling, but you see it wasn't in your bureau at all. I found it in your wardrobe shelf."

"Why, isn't that too extraordinary? I could have declared I put it in that bureau drawer. I do think it's fortunate that I've never had to give evidence in a court case. I'd just worry myself to death in case I wasn't remembering a thing just right."

Mr. Gardener said:

" Mrs. Gardener is very conscientious."

5

It was some five minutes later that Patrick Redfern said:

" Going for your row this morning, Miss Brewster? Mind if I come with you?"

Miss Brewster said heartily:

" Delighted."

" Let's row right round the island," proposed Redfern.

Miss Brewster consulted her watch.

" Shall we have time? Oh yes, it's not half-past eleven yet. Come on, then, let's start."

They went down the beach together.

Patrick Redfern took first turn at the oars. He rowed with a powerful stroke. The boat leapt forward.

Emily Brewster said approvingly:

" Good. We'll see if you can keep that up."

He laughed into her eyes. His spirits had improved.

" I shall probably have a fine crop of blisters by the time we get back." He threw up his head, tossing back his black hair. " God, it's a marvellous day! If you do get a real summer's day in England there's nothing to beat it."

Emily Brewster said gruffly:

" Can't beat England anyway in my opinion. Only place in the world to live in."

" I'm with you."

They rounded the point of the bay to the west and rowed under the cliffs. Patrick Redfern looked up.

" Any one on Sunny Ledge this morning? Yes, there's a sunshade. Who is it, I wonder?"

Emily Brewster said:

" It's Miss Darnley, I think. She's got one of those Japanese affairs."

They rowed up the coast. On their left was the open sea.

Emily Brewster said:

" We ought to have gone the other way round. This way we've got the current against us."

"There's very little current. I've swum out here and not noticed it. Anyway we couldn't go the other way, the causeway wouldn't be covered."

"Depends on the tide, of course. But they always say that bathing from Pixy Cove is dangerous if you swim out too far."

Patrick was rowing vigorously still. At the same time he was scanning the cliffs attentively.

Emily Brewster thought suddenly:

"He's looking for the Marshall woman. That's why he wanted to come with me. She hasn't shown up this morning and he's wondering what she's up to. Probably she's done it on purpose. Just a move in the game—to make him keener."

They rounded the jutting point of rock to the south of the little bay named Pixy's Cove. It was quite a small cove, with rocks dotted fantastically about the beach. It faced nearly north-west and the cliff overhung it a good deal. It was a favourite place for picnic teas. In the morning, when the sun was off it, it was not popular and there was seldom any one there.

On this occasion, however, there was a figure on the beach. Patrick Redfern's stroke checked and recovered.

He said in a would-be casual tone:

"Hullo, who's that?"

Miss Brewster said dryly:

"It looks like Mrs. Marshall."

Patrick Redfern said, as though struck by the idea,

"So it does."

He altered his course, rowing inshore.

Emily Brewster protested.

"We don't want to land here, do we?"

Patrick Redfern said quickly:

"Oh, plenty of time."

His eyes looked into hers—something in them, a naïve pleading look rather like that of an importunate dog, silenced Emily Brewster. She thought to herself:

"Poor boy, he's got it badly. Oh well, it can't be helped. He'll get over it in time."

The boat was fast approaching the beach.

Arlena Marshall was lying face downwards on the shingle, her arms outstretched. The white float was drawn up near-by.

Something was puzzling Emily Brewster. It was as though

she was looking at something she knew quite well but which was in one respect quite wrong.

It was a minute or two before it came to her.

Arlena Marshall's attitude was the attitude of a sun-bather. So had she lain many a time on the beach by the hotel, her bronzed body outstretched and the green cardboard hat protecting her head and neck.

But there was no sun on Pixy's Beach and there would be none for some hours yet. The overhanging cliff protected the beach from the sun in the morning. A vague feeling of apprehension came over Emily Brewster.

The boat grounded on the shingle. Patrick Redfern called: "Hullo, Arlena."

And then Emily Brewster's foreboding took definite shape. For the recumbent figure did not move or answer.

Emily saw Patrick Redfern's face change. He jumped out of the boat and she followed him. They dragged the boat ashore then set off up the beach to where that white figure lay so still and unresponsive near the bottom of the cliff.

Patrick Redfern got there first but Emily Brewster was close behind him.

She saw, as one sees in a dream, the bronzed limbs, the white backless bathing-dress—the red curl of hair escaping under the jade-green hat—saw something else too—the curious unnatural angle of the outspread arms. Felt, in that minute, that this body had not *lain* down but had been *thrown*. . .

She heard Patrick's voice—a mere frightened whisper. He knelt down beside that still form—touched the hand—the arm. . . .

He said in a low shuddering whisper:
"*My God, she's dead. . . .*"
And then, as he lifted the hat a little, peered at the neck:
"*Oh, God, she's been strangled . . . murdered.*"

6

It was one of those moments when time stands still.

With an odd feeling of unreality Emily Brewster heard herself saying:

"We mustn't touch anything. . . . Not until the police come."

Redfern's answer came mechanically.

"No—no—of course not." And then in a deep agonised whisper. "Who? *Who?* Who could have done that to Arlena. She can't have—have been murdered. It can't be true!"

Emily Brewster shook her head, not knowing quite what to answer.

She heard him draw in his breath—heard the low controlled rage in his voice as he said.

"My God, if I get my hands on the foul fiend who did this."

Emily Brewster shivered. Her imagination pictured a lurking murderer behind one of the boulders. Then she heard her voice saying:

"Whoever did it wouldn't be hanging about. We must get the police. Perhaps—" she hesitated—"one of us ought to stay with—with the body."

Patrick Redfern said:

"I'll stay."

Emily Brewster drew a little sigh of relief. She was not the kind of woman who would ever admit to feeling fear, but she was secretly thankful not to have to remain on that beach alone with the faint possibility of a homicidal maniac lingering close at hand.

She said:

"Good. I'll be as quick as I can. I'll go in the boat. Can't face that ladder. There's a constable at Leathercombe Bay."

Patrick Redfern murmured mechanically:

"Yes—yes, whatever you think best."

As she rowed vigorously away from the shore, Emily Brewster saw Patrick drop down beside the dead woman and bury his head in his hands. There was something so forlorn about his attitude that she felt an unwilling sympathy. He looked like a dog watching by its dead master. Nevertheless her robust common sense was saying to her:

"Best thing that could have happened for him and his wife—and for Marshall and the child—but I don't suppose *he* can see it that way, poor devil."

Emily Brewster was a woman who could always rise to an emergency.

Chapter Five

1

INSPECTOR COLGATE stood back by the cliff waiting for the police-surgeon to finish with Arlena's body. Patrick Redfern and Emily Brewster stood a little to one side.

Dr. Neasdon rose from his knees with a quick deft movement.

He said:

" Strangled—and by a pretty powerful pair of hands. She doesn't seem to have put up much of a struggle. Taken by surprise. H'm—well—nasty business."

Emily Brewster had taken one look and then quickly averted her eyes from the dead woman's face. That horrible purple convulsed countenance.

Inspector Colgate asked:

" What about time of death?"

Neasdon said irritably:

"Can't say definitely without knowing more about her. Lots of factors to take into account. Let's see, it's quarter to one now. What time was it when you found her?"

Patrick Redfern, to whom the question was addressed, said vaguely:

"Some time before twelve. I don't know exactly."

Emily Brewster said:

" It was exactly a quarter to twelve when we found she was dead."

" Ah, and you came here in the boat. What time was it when you caught sight of her lying here?"

Emily Brewster considered.

" I should say we rounded the point about five or six minutes earlier." She turned to Redfern. " Do you agree?"

He said vaguely:

" Yes—yes—about that, I should think."

Neasdon asked the Inspector in a low voice:

" This the husband? Oh! I see, my mistake. Thought it might be. He seems rather done in over it."

He raised his voice officially.

"Let's put it at twenty minutes to twelve. She cannot have been killed very long before that. Say between then and eleven—quarter to eleven at the earliest outside limit."

The Inspector shut his notebook with a snap.

"Thanks," he said. "That ought to help us considerably. Puts it within very narrow limits—less than an hour all told."

He turned to Miss Brewster.

"Now then, I think it's all clear so far. You're Miss Emily Brewster and this is Mr. Patrick Redfern, both staying at the Jolly Roger Hotel. You identify this lady as a fellow guest of yours at the hotel—the wife of a Captain Marshall?"

Emily Brewster nodded.

"Then. I think," said Inspector Colgate, "that we'll adjourn to the hotel."

He beckoned to a constable.

"Hawkes, you stay here and don't allow any one on to this cove. I'll be sending Phillips along later."

2

"Upon my soul!" said Colonel Weston. "This is a surprise finding you here!"

Hercule Poirot replied to the Chief Constable's greeting in a suitable manner. He murmured:

"Ah, yes, many years have passed since that affair at St. Loo."

"I haven't forgotten it, though," said Weston. "Biggest surprise of my life. The thing I've never got over, though, is the way you got round me about that funeral business. Absolutely unorthodox, the whole thing. Fantastic!"

"*Tout de même, mon Colonel,*" said Poirot. "It produced the goods, did it not?"

"Er—well, possibly. I dare say we should have got there by more orthodox methods."

"It is possible," agreed Poirot diplomatically.

"And here you are in the thick of another murder," said the Chief Constable. "Any ideas about this one?"

Poirot said slowly:

"Nothing definite—but it is interesting."

"Going to give us a hand?"

"You would permit it, yes?"

" My dear fellow, delighted to have you. Don't know enough yet to decide whether it's a case for Scotland Yard or not. Off-hand it looks as though our murderer must be pretty well within a limited radius. On the other hand, all these people are strangers down here. To find out about them and their motives you've got to go to London."

Poirot said :

" Yes, that is true."

" First of all," said Weston, " we've got to find out who last saw the dead woman alive. Chambermaid took her her breakfast at nine. Girl in the bureau downstairs saw her pass through the lounge and go out about ten."

" My friend," said Poirot, " I suspect that I am the man you want."

" You saw her this morning? What time?"

" At five minutes past ten. I assisted her to launch her float from the bathing beach."

" And she went off on it?"

" Yes."

" Alone?"

" Yes."

" Did you see which direction she took?"

" She paddled round that point there to the right."

" In the direction of Pixy's Cove, that is?"

" Yes."

" And the time then was——?"

" I should say she actually left the beach at a quarter past ten."

Weston considered.

" That fits in well enough. How long should you say that it would take her to paddle round to the Cove?"

" Ah me, I am not an expert. I do not go in boats or expose myself on floats. Perhaps half an hour?"

" That's about what I think," said the Colonel. " She wouldn't be hurrying, I presume. Well, if she arrived there at a quarter to eleven, that fits in well enough."

" At what time does your doctor suggest she died?"

" Oh, Neasden doesn't commit himself. He's a cautious chap. A quarter to eleven is his earliest outside limit."

Poirot nodded. He said :

" There is one other point that I must mention. As she left, Mrs. Marshall asked me not to say I had seen her."

Weston stared.

He said:

"H'm, that's rather suggestive, isn't it?"

Poirot murmured.

"Yes. I thought so myself."

Weston tugged at his moustache. He said:

"Look here, Poirot. You're a man of the world. What sort of a woman was Mrs. Marshall?"

A faint smile came to Poirot's lips.

He asked:

"Have you not already heard?"

The Chief Constable said dryly:

"I know what the women say of her. They would. How much truth is there in it? *Was* she having an affair with this fellow Redfern?"

"I should say undoubtedly *yes.*"

"He followed her down here. eh?"

"There is reason to suppose so."

"And the husband? Did he know about it? What did he feel?"

Poirot said slowly:

"It is not easy to know what Captain Marshall feels or thinks. He is a man who does not display his emotions."

Weston said sharply:

"But he might have 'em, all the same."

Poirot nodded. He said:

"Oh yes, he might have them."

3

The Chief Constable was being as tactful as it was in his nature to be with Mrs. Castle.

Mrs. Castle was the owner and proprietress of the Jolly Roger Hotel. She was a woman of forty odd with a large bust, rather violent henna red hair, and an almost offensively refined manner of speech.

She was saying:

"That such a thing should happen in my hotel! Ay am sure it has always been the quayettest place imaginable! The people who come here are such naice people. No *rowdiness—*

if you know what ay mean. Not like the big hotels in St. Loo."

"Quite so, Mrs. Castle," said Colonel Weston. "But accidents happen in the best regulated—er households."

"Ay'm sure Inspector Colgate will bear me out," said Mrs. Castle, sending an appealing glance towards the Inspector who was sitting looking very official. "As to the lay censing laws, ay am *most* particular. There has never been *any* irregularity!"

"Quite, quite," said Weston. "We're not blaming you in any way, Mrs. Castle."

"But it does so reflect upon an establishment," said Mrs. Castle, her large bust heaving. "When ay think of the noisy gaping crowds. Of course no one but hotel guests are allowed upon the island—but all the same they will no doubt come and *point* from the shore."

She shuddered.

Inspector Colgate saw his chance to turn the conversation to good account.

He said:

"In regard to that point you've just raised. Access to the island. How do you keep people off?"

"Ay am *most* particular about it."

"Yes, but what measures do you take? *What* keeps 'em off? Holiday crowds in summer time swarm everywhere like flies."

Mrs. Castle shrugged slightly again.

She said:

"That is the fault of the charabancs. Ay have seen eighteen at one time parked by the quay at Leathercombe Bay. Eighteen!"

"Just so. How do you stop them coming here?"

"There are notices. And then, of course, at high tide, we are cut off."

"Yes, but at low tide?"

Mrs. Castle explained. At the island end of the causeway there was a gate. This said "Jolly Roger Hotel. Private. No entry except to Hotel." The rocks rose sheer out of the sea on either side there and could not be climbed.

"Any one could take a boat, though, I suppose, and row round and land on one of the coves? You couldn't stop them doing that. There's a right of access to the foreshore. You can't stop people being on the beach between low and high watermark."

But this, it seemed, very seldom happened. Boats could be obtained at Leathercombe Bay harbour, but from there it was a long row to the island, and there was also a strong current just outside Leathercombe Bay harbour.

There were notices, too, on both Gull Cove and Pixy Cove by the ladder. She added that George or William were always on the look out at the bathing beach proper which was the nearest to the mainland.

" Who are George and William?"

" George attends to the bathing beach. He sees to the costumes and the floats. William is the gardener. He keeps the paths and marks the tennis courts and all that."

Colonel Weston said impatiently:

" Well, that seems clear enough. That's not to say that nobody could have come from outside, but any one who did so took a risk—the risk of being noticed. We'll have a word with George and William presently."

Mrs. Castle said:

" Ay do not care for trippers—a very noisy crowd, and they frequently leave orange peel and cigarette boxes on the causeway and down by the rocks, but all the same ay never thought one of them would turn out to be a murderer. Oh dear! it really is too terrible for words. A lady like Mrs. Marshall murdered and what's so horrible, actually—er—strangled . . ."

Mrs. Castle could hardly bring herself to say the word. She brought it out with the utmost reluctance.

Inspector Colgate said soothingly:

" Yes, it's a nasty business."

" And the newspapers. *My* hotel in the newspapers!' "

Colgate said, with a faint grin.

" Oh well, it's advertisment, in a way."

Mrs. Castle drew herself up. Her bust heaved and whalebone creaked. She said icily:

" That is not the kind of advertisement ay care about, Mr. Colgate."

Colonel Weston broke in. He said:

" Now then, Mrs. Castle. you've got a list of the guests staying here, as I asked you?"

"Yes, sir."

Colonel Weston pored over the hotel register. He looked over to Poirot who made the fourth member of the group assembled in the manageress's office.

"This is where you'll probably be able to help us presently."

He read down the names.

"What about servants?"

Mrs. Castle produced a second list.

"There are four chambermaids, the head waiter and three under him and Henry in the bar. William does the boots and shoes. Then there's the cook and two under her."

"What about the waiters?"

"Well, sir, Albert, the Mater Dotel, came to me from the Vincent at Plymouth. He was there for some years. The three under him have been here for three years—one of them four. They are very naise lads and most respectable. Henry has been here since the hotel opened. He is quite an institution."

Weston nodded. He said to Colgate:

"Seems all right. You'll check up on them, of course. Thank you, Mrs. Castle."

"That will be all you require?"

"For the moment, yes."

Mrs. Castle creaked out of the room.

Weston said:

"First thing to do is to talk with Captain Marshall.

4

Kenneth Marshall sat quietly answering the questions put to him. Apart from a slight hardening of his features he was quite calm. Seen here, with the sunlight falling on him from the window, you realised that he was a handsome man. Those straight features, the steady blue eyes, the firm mouth. His voice was low and pleasant.

Colonel Weston was saying:

"I quite understand, Captain Marshall, what a terrible shock this must be to you. But you realise that I am anxious to get the fullest information as soon as possible."

Marshall nodded.

He said:

"I quite understand. Carry on."

" Mrs. Marshall was your second wife?"

" Yes."

" And you have been married how long?"

" Just over four years."

" And her name before she was married?"

" Helen Stuart. Her acting name was Arlena Stuart."

" She was an actress?"

" She appeared in Revue and musical shows."

" Did she give up the stage on her marriage?"

" No. She continued to appear. She actually retired only about a year and a half ago."

" Was there any special reason for her retirement?"

Kenneth Marshall appeared to consider.

" No," he said. " She simply said that she was tired of it all."

" It was not—er—in obedience to your special wish?"

Marshall raised his eyebrows.

" Oh, no."

" You were quite content for her to continue acting after your marriage?"

Marshall smiled very faintly.

" I should have preferred her to give it up—that, yes. But I made no fuss about it."

" It caused no point of dissension between you?"

" Certainly not. My wife was free to please herself."

" And—the marriage was a happy one?"

Kenneth Marshall said coldly:

" Certainly."

Colonel Weston paused a minute. Then he said:

" Captain Marshall, have you any idea who could possibly have killed your wife?"

The answer came without the least hesitation.

" None whatever."

" Had she any enemies?"

" Possibly."

" Ah?"

The other went on quickly. He said:

" Don't misunderstand me, sir. My wife was an actress. She was also a very good-looking woman. In both capacities she aroused a certain amount of jealousy and envy. There were fusses over parts—there was rivalry from other women —there was a good deal, shall we say, of general envy, hatred, malice, and all uncharitableness! But that is not to say that there was any one who was capable of deliberately murdering her."

Hercule Poirot spoke for the first time. He said:

"What you really mean, Monsieur, is that her enemies were mostly or entirely, *women*?"

Kenneth Marshall looked across at him.

"Yes," he said. "That is so."

The Chief Constable said:

"You know of no man who had a grudge against her?"

"No."

"Was she previously acquainted with any one in this hotel?"

"I believe she had met Mr. Redfern before—at some cocktail party. Nobody else to my knowledge."

Weston paused. He seemed to deliberate as to whether to pursue the subject. Then he decided against that course. He said:

"We now come to this morning. When was the last time you saw your wife?"

Marshall paused a minute, then he said:

"I looked in on my way down to breakfast——"

"Excuse me, you occupied separate rooms?"

"Yes."

"And what time was that?"

"It must have been about nine o'clock."

"What was she doing?"

"She was opening her letters."

"Did she say anything?"

"Nothing of any particular interest. Just good-morning—and that it was a nice day—that sort of thing."

"What was her manner? Unusual at all?"

"No, perfectly normal."

"She did not seem excited, or depressed, or upset in any way?"

"I certainly didn't notice it."

Hercule Poirot said:

"Did she mention at all what were the contents of her letters?"

Again a faint smile appeared on Marshall's lips. He said:

"As far as I can remember, she said they were all bills."

"Your wife breakfasted in bed?"

c

"Yes."

"Did she always do that?"

"Invariably."

Hercule Poirot said:

"What time did she usually come downstairs?"

"Oh! between ten and eleven—usually nearer eleven."

Poriot went on:

"If she was to descend at ten o'clock exactly, that would be rather surprising?"

"Yes. She wasn't often down as early as that."

"But she was this morning. Why do you think that was, Captain Marshall?"

Marshall said unemotionally:

"Haven't the least idea. Might have been the weather— extra fine day and all that."

"You missed her?"

Kenneth Marshall shifted a little in his chair. He said:

"Looked in on her again after breakfast. Room was empty. I was a bit surprised."

"And then you came down on the beach and asked me if I had seen her?"

"Er—yes." He added with a faint emphasis in his voice. "And you said you hadn't . . ."

The innocent eyes of Hercule Poirot did not falter. Gently he caressed his large and flamboyant moustache.

Weston asked:

"Had you any special reason for wanting to find your wife this morning?"

Marshall shifted his glance amiably to the Chief Constable. He said:

"No, just wondered where she was, that's all."

Weston paused. He moved his chair slightly. His voice fell into a different key. He said:

"Just now, Captain Marshall, you mentioned that your wife had a previous acquaintance with Mr. Patrick Redfern. How well did your wife know Mr. Redfern?"

Kenneth Marshall said:

"Mind if I smoke?" He felt through his pockets. "Dash! I've mislaid my pipe somewhere."

Poirot offered him a cigarette which he accepted. Lighting it, he said:

"You were asking about Redfern. My wife told me she had come across him at some cocktail party or other."

"He was, then, just a casual acquaintance?"

"I believe so."

"Since then——" the Chief Constable paused. "I understand that that acquaintanceship has ripened into something rather closer."

Marshall said sharply:

"You understand that, do you? Who told you so?"

"It is the common gossip of the hotel."

For a moment Marshall's eyes went to Hercule Poirot. They dwelt on him with a kind of cold anger. He said:

"Hotel gossip is usually a tissue of lies!"

"Possibly. But I gather that Mr. Redfern and your wife gave some grounds for the gossip."

"What grounds?"

"They were constantly in each other's company."

"Is that all?"

"You do not deny that that was so?"

"May have been. I really didn't notice."

"You did not—excuse me, Captain Marshall—object to your wife's friendship with Mr. Redfern?"

"I wasn't in the habit of criticising my wife's conduct."

"You did not protest or object in any way?"

"Certainly not."

"Not even though it was becoming a subject of scandal and an estrangement was growing up between Mr. Redfern and his wife?"

Kenneth Marshall said coldly:

"I mind my own business and I expect other people to mind theirs. I don't listen to gossip and tittle tattle."

"You won't deny that Mr. Redfern admired your wife?"

"He probably did. Most men did. She was a very beautiful woman."

"But you yourself were persuaded that there was nothing serious in the affair?"

"I never thought about it, I tell you."

"And suppose we have a witness who can testify that they were on terms of the greatest intimacy?"

Again those blue eyes went to Hercule Poirot. Again an expression of dislike showed on that usually impassive face.

Marshall said:

"If you want to listen to these tales, listen to 'em. My wife's dead and can't defend herself."

"You mean that you, personally, don't believe them?"

For the first time a faint dew of sweat was observable on Marshall's brow. He said:

"I don't propose to believe anything of the kind."

He went on:

"Aren't you getting a good way from the essentials of this business? What I believe or don't believe is surely not relevant to the plain fact of murder?"

Hercule Poirot answered before either of the others could speak. He said:

"You do not comprehend, Captain Marshall. There is no such thing as a plain fact of murder. Murder springs, nine times out of ten, out of the character and circumstances of the murdered person. *Because* the victim was the kind of person he or she was, *therefore* was he or she murdered! Until we can understand fully and completely *exactly what kind of a person Arlena Marshall was*, we shall not be able to see clearly exactly *the kind of person who murdered her*. From that springs the necessity of our questions."

Marshall turned to the Chief Constable. He said:

"That your view, too?"

Weston boggled a little. He said:

"Well, up to a point—that is to say——"

Marshall gave a short laugh. He said:

"Thought you wouldn't agree. This character stuff is M. Poirot's speciality, I believe."

Poirot said, smiling:

"You can at least congratulate yourself on having done nothing to assist me!"

"What do you mean?"

"What have you told us about your wife? Exactly nothing at all. You have told us only what every one could see for themselves. That she was beautiful and admired. Nothing more."

Kenneth Marshall shrugged his shoulders. He said simply:

"You're crazy."

He looked towards the Chief Constable and said with emphasis:

"Anything else, sir, that *you'd* like me to tell you?"

"Yes, Captain Marshall, your own movements this morning, please."

Kenneth Marshall nodded. He had clearly expected this.

He said:

"I breakfasted downstairs about nine o'clock as usual and read the paper. As I told you I went up to my wife's room afterwards and found she had gone out. I came down to the beach, saw M. Poirot and asked if he had seen her. Then I had a quick bathe and went up to the hotel again. It was then, let me see, about twenty to eleven—yes, just about that. I saw the clock in the lounge. It was just after twenty minutes to. I went up to my room, but the chambermaid hadn't quite finished it. I asked her to finish as quickly as she could. I had some letters to type which I wanted to get off by the post. I went downstairs again and had a word or two with Henry in the bar. I went up again to my room at ten minutes to eleven. There I typed my letters. I typed until ten minutes to twelve. I then changed into tennis kit as I had a date to play tennis at twelve. We'd booked the court the day before."

"Who was we?"

"Mrs. Redfern, Miss Darnley, Mr. Gardener and myself. I came down at twelve o'clock and went up to the court. Miss Darnley was there and Mr. Gardener. Mrs. Redfern arrived a few minutes later. We played tennis for an hour. Just as we came into the hotel afterwards I—I—got the news."

"Thank you, Captain Marshall. Just as a matter of form, is there any one who can corroborate the fact that you were typing in your room between—er—ten minutes to eleven and ten minutes to twelve?"

Kenneth Marshall said with a faint smile:

"Have you got some idea that I killed my own wife? Let me see now. The chambermaid was about doing the rooms. She must have heard the typewriter going. And then there are the letters themselves. With all this upset I haven't posted them. I should imagine they are as good evidence as anything."

He took three letters from his pocket. They were addressed, but not stamped. He said:

"Their contents, by the way, are strictly confidential. But when it's a case of murder, one is forced to trust in the discretion of the police. They contain lists of figures and various financial statements. I think you will find that if you put one of your men on to type them out, he won't do it in much under an hour."

He paused.

" Satisfied, I hope?"

Weston said smoothly.

" It is no question of suspicion. Every one on the island will be asked to account for his or her movements between a quarter to eleven and twenty minutes to twelve this morning."

Kenneth Marshall said:

" Quite."

Weston said:

" One more thing, Captain Marshall. Do you know anything about the way your wife was likely to have disposed of any property she had?"

" You mean a will? I don't think she ever made a will."

" But you are not sure?"

" Her solicitors are Barkett, Markett & Applegood, Bedford Square. They saw to all her contracts, etc. But I'm fairly certain she never made a will. She said once that doing a thing like that would give her the shivers."

" In that case, if she has died intestate, you, as her husband, succeed to her property."

" Yes, I suppose I do."

" Had she any near relatives?"

" I don't think so. If she had, she never mentioned them. I know that her father and mother died when she was a child and she had no brothers or sisters."

" In any case, I suppose, she had nothing very much to leave?"

Kenneth Marshall said coolly:

" On the contrary. Only two years ago, Sir Robert Erskine who was an old friend of hers, died and left her most of his fortune. It amounted, I think, to about fifty thousand pounds."

Inspector Colgate looked up. An alertness came into his glance. Up to now he had been silent. Now he asked:

" Then actually, Captain Marshall, your wife was a rich woman?"

Kenneth Marshall shrugged his shoulders.

" I suppose she was really."

" And you still say she did not make a will?"

" You can ask the solicitors. But I'm pretty certain she didn't. As I tell you, she thought it unlucky."

There was a pause then Marshall added:

" Is there anything further?"

Weston shook his head.

" Don't think so—eh Colgate? No. Once more, Captain Marshall, let me offer you all my sympathy in your loss."

Marshall blinked. He said jerkily:

" Oh—thanks."

He went out.

5

The three men looked at each other.

Weston said:

" Cool customer. Not giving anything away, is he? What do you make of him, Colgate?"

The Inspector shook his head.

" It's difficult to tell. He's not the kind that shows anything. That sort makes a bad impression in the witness-box, and yet it's a bit unfair on them really. Sometimes they're as cut up as anything and yet can't show it. That kind of manner made the jury bring in a verdict of Guilty against Wallace. It wasn't the evidence. They just couldn't believe that a man could lose his wife and talk and act so coolly about it."

Weston turned to Poirot.

" What do you think, Poirot?"

Hercule Poirot raised his hands.

He said:

" What can one say? He is the closed box—the fastened oyster. He has chosen his rôle. He has heard nothing, he has seen nothing, he knows nothing!"

" We've got a choice of motives," said Colgate. " There's jealousy and there's the money motive. Of course, in a way, a husband's the obvious suspect. One naturally thinks of him first. If he knew his missus was carrying on with the other chap——"

Poirot interrupted.

He said:

" I think he knew that."

"Why do you say so?"

"Listen, my friend. Last night I had been talking with Mrs. Redfern on Sunny Ledge. I came down from there to the hotel and on my way I saw those two together—Mrs. Marshall and Patrick Redfern. And a moment or two after I met Captain Marshall. His face was very stiff. It says nothing—but nothing at all! It is almost *too* blank, if you understand me. Oh! he knew all right."

Colgate grunted doubtfully.

He said:

"Oh well, if you think so——"

"I am sure of it! But even then, what does that tell us? What did Kenneth Marshall *feel* about his wife?"

Colonel Weston said:

"Takes her death coolly enough."

Poirot shook his head in a dissatisfied manner.

Inspector Colgate said:

"Sometimes these quiet ones are the most violent underneath, so to speak. It's all bottled up. He may have been madly fond of her—and madly jealous. But he's not the kind to show it."

Poirot said slowly:

"That is possible—yes. He is a very interesting character this Captain Marshall. I interest myself in him greatly. And in his *alibi*."

"Alibi by typewriter," said Weston with a short bark of a laugh. "What have you got to say about that, Colgate?"

Inspector Colgate screwed up his eyes. He said:

"Well, you know, sir, I rather fancy that alibi. It's not too good, if you know what I mean. It's—well, it's *natural*. And if we find the chambermaid was about, and did hear the typewriter going, well then, it seems to me that it's all right and that we'll have to look elsewhere."

"H'm," said Colonel Weston. "Where are you going to look?"

6

For a minute or two the three men pondered the question. Inspector Colgate spoke first. He said:

"It boils down to this—was it an outsider, or a guest at the hotel? I'm not eliminating the servants entirely, mind, but I don't expect for a minute that we'll find any of them had a hand in it. No, it's a hotel guest, or it's someone from right outside. We've got to look at it this way. First of all—motive. There's gain. The only person to gain by her death was the lady's husband, it seems. What other motives are there? First and foremost—jealousy. It seems to me—just looking at it—that if ever you've got a *crime passionnel*—(he bowed to Poirot) this is one."

Poirot murmured as he looked up at the ceiling:

"There are so many passions."

Inspector Colgate went on:

"Her husband wouldn't allow that she had any enemies—real enemies, that is, but I don't believe for a minute that that's so! I should say that a lady like her would—well, would make some pretty bad enemies—eh, sir, what do you say?"

Poirot responded. He said:

"*Mais oui*, that is so. Arlena Marshall would make enemies. But in my opinion, the enemy theory is not tenable, for you see, Inspector, Arlena Marshall's enemies would, I think, as I said just now, always be *women*."

Colonel Weston grunted and said:

"Something in that. It's the women who've got their knife into her here all right."

Poirot went on.

"It seems to be hardly possible that this crime was committed by a woman. What does the medical evidence say?"

Weston grunted again. He said:

"Neasdon's pretty confident that she was strangled by a man. Big hands—powerful grip. It's just possible, of course, that an unusually athletic woman might have done it—but it's damned unlikely."

Poirot nodded.

"Exactly. Arsenic in a cup of tea—a box of poisoned chocolates—a knife—even a pistol—but strangulation—no! It is a man we have to look for."

"And immediately," he went on, "it becomes more difficult. There are two people here in this hotel who have a motive for wishing Arlena Marshall out of the way— but both of them are women."

Colonel Weston asked:

" Redfern's wife is one of them, I suppose?"

" Yes. Mrs. Redfern might have made up her mind to kill Arlena Stuart. She had, let us say, ample cause. I think, too, that it would be possible for Mrs. Redfern to commit a murder. But not this kind of murder. For all her unhappiness and jealousy, she is not, I should say, a woman of strong passions. In love, she would be devoted and loyal—not passionate. As I said just now—arsenic in the teacup, possibly—strangulation, no. I am sure, also, that she is physically incapable of committing this crime, her hands and feet are small, below the average."

Weston nodded. He said:

" This isn't a woman's crime. No, a man did this."

Inspector Colgate coughed.

" Let me put forward a solution, sir. Say that prior to meeting this Mr. Redfern the lady had had another affair with someone—call him X. She turns X down for Mr. Redfern. X is mad with rage and jealousy. He follows her down here, stays somewhere in the neighbourhood, comes over to the island does her in. It's a possibility!"

Weston said:

" It's *possible*, all right. And if it's true, it ought to be easy to prove. Did he come on foot or in a boat? The latter seems more likely. If so, he must have hired a boat somewhere. You'd better make inquiries."

He looked across at Poirot.

" What do you think of Colgate's suggestion?"

Poirot said slowly:

" It leaves, somehow, too much to chance. And besides—somewhere the picture is not true. I cannot, you see, imagine this man . . . the man who is mad with rage and jealousy."

Colgate said:

" People *did* go potty about her, though, sir. Look at Redfern."

" Yes, yes ; . . But all the same——"

Colgate looked at him questioningly.

Poirot shook his head.

He said, frowning:

" Somewhere, there is something that we have missed. . . ."

Chapter Six

1

COLONEL WESTON was poring over the hotel register.
He read aloud:
" Major and Mrs. Cowan,
Miss Pamela Cowan,
Master Robert Cowan,
Master Evan Cowan,
　　Rydal's Mount, Leatherhead.
Mr. and Mrs. Masterman,
Mr. Edward Masterman,
Miss Jennifer Masterman,
Mr Roy Masterman,
Master Frederick Masterman,
　　5 Marlborough Avenue, London, N.W.
Mr. and Mrs. Gardener,
　　New York.
Mr. and Mrs. Redfern,
　　Crossgates, Seldon, Princes Risborough.
Major Barry,
　　18 Cardon St., St. James, London, S.W.1.
Mr. Horace Blatt,
　　5 Pickersgill Street, London, E.C.2.
M. Hercule Poirot,
　　Whitehaven Mansions, London, W.1.
Miss Rosamund Darnley,
　　8 Cardigan Court, W.1.
Miss Emily Brewster,
　　Southgates, Sunbury-on-Thames.
Rev. Stephen Lane,
　　London.
Captain and Mrs. Marshall,
Miss Linda Marshall,
　　73 Upcott Mansions, London, S.W.7."
He stopped.
Inspector Colgate said:
" I think, sir, that we can wash out the first two entries.

Mrs. Castle tells me that the Mastermans and the Cowans come here regularly every summer with their children. This morning they went off on an all-day excursion sailing, taking lunch with them. They left just after nine o'clock. A man called Andrew Baston took them. We can check up from him, but I think we can put them right out of it."

Weston nodded.

"I agree. Let's eliminate every one we can. Can you give us a pointer on any of the rest of them, Poirot?"

Poirot said:

"Superficially, that is easy. The Gardeners are a middle-aged married couple, pleasant, travelled. All the talking is done by the lady. The husband is acquiescent. He plays tennis and golf and has a form of dry humour that is attractive when one gets him to oneself."

"Sounds quite O.K."

"Next—the Redferns. Mr. Redfern is young, attractive to women, a magnificent swimmer, a good tennis player and accomplished dancer. His wife I have already spoken of to you. She is quiet, pretty in a washed-out way. She is, I think, devoted to her husband. She has something that Arlena Marshall did not have."

"What is that?"

"Brains."

Inspector Colgate sighed. He said:

"Brains don't count for much when it comes to an infatuation, sir."

"Perhaps not. And yet I do truly believe that in spite of his infatuation for Mrs. Marshall, Patrick Redfern really cares for his wife."

"That may be, sir. It wouldn't be the first time that's happened."

Poirot murmured.

"That is the pity of it! It is always the thing women find hardest to believe."

He went on:

"Major Barry. Retired Indian Army. An admirer of women. A teller of long and boring stories."

Inspector Colgate sighed.

"You needn't go on. I've met a few, sir."

"Mr. Horace Blatt. He is, apparently, a rich man. He talks a good deal—about Mr. Blatt. He wants to be everybody's friend. It is sad For nobody likes him very much. And there is something else. Mr. Blatt last night asked me a good many questions. Mr. Blatt was uneasy. Yes, there is something not quite right about Mr. Blatt."

He paused and went on with a change of voice:

"Next comes Miss Rosamund Darnley. Her business name is Rose Mond Ltd. She is a celebrated dressmaker. What can I say of her? She has brains and charm and chic. She is very pleasing to look at." He paused and added. "And she is a very old friend of Captain Marshall's."

Weston sat up in his chair.

"Oh, she is, is she?"

"Yes. They had not met for some years."

Weston asked:

"Did she know he was going to be down here?"

"She says not."

Poirot paused and then went on.

"Who comes next? Miss Brewster. I find her just a little alarming." He shook his head. "She has a voice like a man's. She is gruff and what you call hearty. She rows boats and has a handicap of four at golf." He paused. "I think, though, that she has a good heart."

Weston said:

"That leaves only the Reverend Stephen Lane. Who's the Reverend Stephen Lane?"

"I can only tell you one thing. He is a man who is in a condition of great nervous tension. Also he is, I think, a fanatic."

Inspector Colgate said:

"Oh, that kind of person."

Weston said:

"And that's the lot!" He looked at Poirot. "You seem very lost in thought, my friend?"

Poirot said:

"Yes. Because, you see, when Mrs. Marshall went off this morning and asked me not to tell any one I had seen her, I jumped at once in my own mind to a certain conclusion. I thought that her friendship with Patrick Redfern had made trouble between her and her husband. I thought that she was going to meet Patrick Redfern somewhere, and that she did not want her husband to know where she was."

He paused.

" But that, you see, was where I was wrong. Because, although her husband appeared almost immediately on the beach and asked if I had seen her, Patrick Redfern arrived also—and was most patently and obviously looking for her! And therefore, my friends, I am asking myself, *who was it that Arlena Marshall went off to meet?*"

Inspector Colgate said:

" That fits in with *my* idea. A man from London or somewhere."

Hercule Poirot shook his head. He said:

" But, my friend, according to your theory, Arlena Marshall had broken with this mythical man. Why, then, should she take such trouble and pains to meet him?"

Inspector Colgate shook his head. He said:

" Why do *you* think it was?"

" That is just what I cannot imagine. We have just read through the list of hotel guests. They are all middle-aged—dull. Which of them would Arlena Marshall prefer to Patrick Redfern? No, that is impossible. And yet, all the same, she *did* go to meet someone—and that someone was not Patrick Redfern."

Weston murmured:

" You don't think she just went off by herself?"

Poirot shook his head.

" *Mon cher,*" he said. " It is very evident that you never met the dead woman. Somebody once wrote a learned treatise on the difference that solitary confinement would mean to Beau Brummel or to a man like Newton. Arlena Marshall, my dear friend, would practically not exist in solitude. She only lived in the light of a man's admiration. No, Arlena Marshall went to meet *someone* this morning. *Who was it?*"

2

Colonel Weston sighed, shook his head and said:

" Well, we can go into theories later. Got to get through these interviews now. Got to get it down in black and white where every one was. I suppose we'd better see the Marshall girl now. She might be able to tell us something useful."

Linda Marshall came into the room clumsily, knocking

against the doorpost. She was breathing quickly and the pupils of her eyes were dilated. She looked like a startled young colt. Colonel Weston felt a kindly impulse towards her.

He thought:

"Poor kid—she's nothing but a kid after all. This must have been a pretty bad shock to her."

He drew up a chair and said in a reassuring voice.

"Sorry to put you through this, Miss—Linda, isn't it?"

"Yes, Linda."

Her voice had that indrawn breathy quality that is often characteristic of schoolgirls. Her hands rested helplessly on the table in front of him—pathetic hands, big and red, with large bones and long wrists. Weston thought:

"A kid oughtn't to be mixed up in this sort of thing."

He said reassuringly.

"There's nothing very alarming about all this. We just want you to tell us anything you know that might be useful, that's all."

Linda said:

"You mean—about Arlena?"

"Yes. Did you see her this morning at all?"

The girl shook her head.

"No. Arlena always gets down rather late. She has breakfast in bed."

Hercule Poirot said:

"And you, Mademoiselle?"

"Oh. I get up. Breakfast in bed's so *stuffy*."

Weston said:

"Will you tell us just what you did this morning?"

"Well, I had a bathe first and then breakfast, and then I went with Mrs. Redfern to Gull Cove."

Weston said:

"What time did you and Mrs. Redfern start?"

"She said she'd be waiting for me in the hall at half-past ten. I was afraid I was going to be late, but it was all right. We started off at about three minutes to the half-hour."

Poirot said:

"And what did you do at Gull Cove?"

"Oh, I oiled myself and sunbathed and Mrs. Redfern sketched. Then, later, I went into the sea and Christine went back to the hotel to get changed for tennis."

Weston said, keeping his voice quite casual:

" Do you remember what time that was?"

" When Mrs. Redfern went back to the hotel? Quarter to twelve."

" Sure of that time—quarter to twelve?"

Linda, opening her eyes wide, said:

" Oh *yes.* I looked at my watch."

" The watch you have on now?"

Linda glanced down at her wrist.

" Yes."

Weston said:

" Mind if I see?"

She held out her wrist. He compared the watch with his own and with the hotel clock on the wall.

He said, smiling:

" Correct to a second. And after that you had a bathe?"

" Yes."

" And you got back to the hotel—when?"

" Just about one o'clock. And—and then—I heard—about Arlena. . . ."

Her voice changed.

Colonel Weston said:

" Did you—er—get on with your stepmother all right?"

She looked at him for a minute without replying. Then she said:

" Oh yes."

Poirot asked:

" Did you like her, Mademoiselle?"

Linda said again:

" Oh yes." She added. " Arlena was quite kind to me."

Weston said with rather uneasy facetiousness.

" Not the cruel stepmother, eh?"

Linda shook her head without smiling.

Weston said:

" That's good. That's good. Sometimes, you know, there's a bit of difficulty in families—jealousy—all that. Girl and her father great pals and then she resents it a bit when he's all wrapped up in the new wife. You didn't feel like that, eh?"

Linda stared at him. She said with obvious sincerity:

" Oh no."

Weston said:

" I suppose your father was—er—very wrapped up in her?"

Linda said simply:

" I don't know."

Weston went on:

" All sorts of difficulties, as I say, arise in families. Quarrels—rows—that sort of thing. If husband and wife get ratty with each other, that's a bit awkward for a daughter too. Anything of that sort?"

Linda said clearly:

" Do you mean, did Father and Arlena quarrel?"

" Well—yes."

Weston thought to himself:

" Rotten business—questioning a child about her father. Why is one a policeman? Damn it all, it's got to be done, though."

Linda said positively:

" Oh no." She added. " Father doesn't quarrel with people. He's not like that at all."

Weston said:

" No, Miss Linda, I want you to think very carefully. Have you any idea at all who might have killed your stepmother? Is there anything you've ever heard or anything you know that could help us on that point?"

Linda was silent a minute. She seemed to be giving the question a serious unhurried consideration. She said at last.

" No, I don't know who could have wanted to kill Arlena." She added: " Except, of course, Mrs. Redfern."

Weston said:

" You think Mrs. Redfern wanted to kill her? Why?"

Linda said:

" Because her husband was in love with Arlena. But I don't think she would really want to *kill* her. I mean she'd just feel that she wished she was dead—and that isn't the same thing at all, is it?"

Poirot said gently:

" No, it is not at all the same."

Linda nodded. A queer sort of spasm passed across her face. She said:

" And anyway, Mrs. Redfern could never do a thing like that—kill anybody. She isn't—she isn't *violent*, if you know what I mean."

Weston and Poirot nodded. The latter said:

" I know exactly what you mean, my child, and I agree with you. Mrs. Redfern is not of those who, as your saying goes, 'sees red.' She would not be "—he leaned back half closing his eyes, picking his words with care—" shaken by a storm of feeling—seeing life narrowing in front of her—seeing a hated face—a hated white neck—feeling her hands clench—longing to feel them press into flesh——"

He stopped.

Linda moved jerkily back from the table. She said in a trembling voice:

"Can I go now? Is that all?"

Colonel Weston said:

"Yes, yes, that's all. Thank you, Miss Linda."

He got up to open the door for her. Then came back to the table and lit a cigarette.

"Phew," he said. "Not a nice job, ours. I can tell you I felt a bit of a cad questioning that child about the relations between her father and her stepmother. More or less inviting a daughter to put a rope round her father's neck. All the same, it had to be done. Murder is murder. And she's the person most likely to know the truth of things. I'm rather thankful, though, that she'd nothing to tell us in that line."

Poirot said:

"Yes, I thought you were."

Weston said with an embarrassed cough:

"By the way, Poirot, you went a bit far, I thought at the end. All that hands sinking into flesh business! Not quite the sort of idea to put into a kid's head."

Hercule Poirot looked at him with thoughtful eyes. He said:

"So you thought I put ideas into her head?"

"Well, didn't you? Come now."

Poirot shook his head.

Weston sheered away from the point. He said:

"On the whole we got very little useful stuff out of her. Except a more or less complete *alibi* for the Redfern woman. If they were together from half-past ten to a quarter to twelve that lets Christine Redfern out of it. Exit the jealous wife suspect."

Poirot said:

"There are better reasons than that for leaving Mrs. Redfern out of it. It would, I am convinced, be physically impossible and mentally impossible for her to strangle any one. She is cold rather than warm blooded, capable of deep devotion and unswerving constancy, but not of hot blooded passion or rage. Moreover, her hands are far too small and delicate."

Colgate said:

"I agree with M. Poirot. She's out of it. Dr. Neasdon says it was a full-sized pair of hands that throttled that dame."

Weston said:

"Well, I suppose we'd better see the Redferns next. I expect he's recovered a bit from the shock now."

3

Patrick Redfern had recovered full composure by now. He looked pale and haggard and suddenly very young, but his manner was quite composed.

"You are Mr. Patrick Redfern of Crossgates, Seldon, Princes Risborough?"

"Yes."

"How long had you known Mrs. Marshall?"

Patrick Redfern hesitated, then said:

"Three months."

Weston went on:

"Captain Marshall has told us that you and she met casually at a cocktail party. Is that right?"

"Yes, that's how it came about."

Weston said:

"Captain Marshall has implied that until you both met down here you did not know each other well. Is that the truth, Mr. Redfern?"

Again Patrick Redfern hesitated a minute. Then he said:

"Well—not exactly. As a matter of fact I saw a fair amount of her one way and another."

"Without Captain Marshall's knowledge?"

Redfern flushed slightly. He said:

"I don't know whether he knew about it or not."

Hercule Poirot spoke. He murmured:

"And was it also without your wife's knowledge, Mr. Redfern?"

"I believe I mentioned to my wife that I had met the famous Arlena Stuart."

Poirot persisted.

" But she did not know how often you were seeing her?"

" Well, perhaps not."

Weston said:

" Did you and Mrs. Marshall arrange to meet down here?"

Redfern was silent a minute or two. Then he shrugged his shoulders.

" Oh well," he said, " I suppose it's bound to come out now. It's no good my fencing with you. I was crazy about the woman—mad—infatuated—anything you like. She wanted me to come down here. I demurred a bit and then I agreed. I—I—well, I would have agreed to do any mortal thing she liked. She had that kind of effect on people."

Hercule Poirot murmured:

" You paint a very clear picture of her. She was the eternal Circe. Just that!"

Patrick Redfern said bitterly:

" She turned men into swine all right!" He went on: " I'm being frank with you, gentlemen. I'm not going to hide anything. What's the use? As I say, I was infatuated with her. Whether she cared for me or not, I don't know. She pretended to, but I think she was one of those women who lose interest in a man once they've got him body and soul. She knew she'd got me all right. This morning, when I found her there on the beach, dead, it was as though "—he paused—" as though something had hit me straight between the eyes. I was dazed—knocked out!"

Poirot leaned forward. " And now?"

Patrick Redfern met his eyes squarely.

He said:

" I've told you the truth. What I want to ask is this—*how much of it has got to be made public?* It's not as though it could have any bearing on her death. And if it all comes out, it's going to be pretty rough on my wife."

" Oh, I know," he went on quickly. " You think I haven't thought much about her up to now? Perhaps that's true. But, though I may sound the worst kind of hypocrite, the real truth is that I care for my wife—care for her very deeply. The other "—he twitched his shoulders—" it was a madness—the kind of idiotic fool thing men do—but Christine is different. She's *real*. Badly as I've treated her, I've known all along, deep down, that she was the person who really counted." He paused—sighed—and said rather pathetically: "I wish I could make you believe that."

Hercule Poirot leant forward. He said:

"But I do believe it. Yes, yes, I do believe it!"

Patrick Redfern looked at him gratefully. He said:

"Thank you."

Colonel Weston cleared his throat. He said:

"You may take it, Mr. Redfern, that we shall not go into irrelevancies. If your infatuation for Mrs. Marshall played no part in the murder then there will be no point in dragging it into the case. But what you don't seem to realise is that that—er—intimacy—may have a very direct bearing on the murder. It might establish, you understand, a *motive* for the crime."

Patrick Redfern said:

"Motive?"

Weston said:

"Yes, Mr. Redfern, *motive*! Captain Marshall, perhaps, was unaware of the affair. Suppose that he suddenly found out?"

Redfern said:

"Oh God! You mean he got wise and—and killed her?"

The Chief Constable said rather dryly:

"That solution had not occurred-to you?"

Redfern shook his head. He said:

"No—funny. I never thought of it. You see, Marshall's such a quiet chap. I—oh, it doesn't seem likely."

Weston asked:

"What was Mrs. Marshall's attitude to her husband in all this? Was she—well, uneasy—in case it should come to his ears? Or was she indifferent?"

Redfern said slowly:

"She was—a bit nervous. She didn't want him to suspect anything."

"Did she seem afraid of him?"

"Afraid No, I wouldn't say that."

Poirot murmured:

"Excuse me, M. Redfern, there was not, at any time, the question of a divorce?"

Patrick Redfern shook his head decisively.

"Oh no, there was no question of anything like that. There

was Christine, you see. And Arlena, I am sure, never thought of such a thing. She was perfectly satisfied married to Marshall. He's—well, rather a big bug in his way——" He smiled suddenly. "County—all that sort of thing, and quite well off. She never thought of me as a possible *husband*. No, I was just one of a succession of poor mutts—just something to pass the time with. I knew that all along, and yet, queerly enough, it didn't alter my feeling towards her . . ."

His voice trailed off. He sat there thinking.

Weston recalled him to the needs of the moment.

"Now, Mr. Redfern, had you any particular appointment with Mrs. Marshall this morning?"

Patrick Redfern looked slightly puzzled.

He said:

"Not a particular appointment, no. We usually met every morning on the beach. We used to paddle about on floats."

"Were you surprised not to find Mrs. Marshall there this morning?"

"Yes, I was. Very surprised. I couldn't understand it at all."

"What did you think?"

"Well, I didn't know what to think. I mean, all the time I thought she would be coming."

"If she were keeping an appointment elsewhere you had no idea with whom that appointment might be?"

Patrick Redfern merely stared and shook his head.

"When you had a *rendezvous* with Mrs. Marshall, where did you meet?"

"Well, sometimes I'd meet her in the afternoon down at Gull Cove. You see the sun is off Gull Cove in the afternoon and so there aren't usually many people there. We met there once or twice."

"Never on the other cove? Pixy Cove?"

"No. You see Pixy Cove faces west and people go round there in boats or on floats in the afternoon. We never tried to meet in the morning. It would have been too noticeable. In the afternoon people go and have a sleep or mouch around and nobody knows much where any one else is."

Weston nodded.

Patrick Redfern went on:

" After dinner, of course, on the fine nights, we used to go off for a stroll together to different parts of the island."

Hercule Poirot murmured:

" Ah, yes!" and Patrick Redfern shot him an inquiring glance.

Weston said:

" Then you can give us no help whatsoever as to the cause that took Mrs. Marshall to Pixy Cove this morning?"

Redfern shook his head. He said, and his voice sounded honestly bewildered:

" I haven't the faintest idea! It wasn't like Arlena."

Weston said:

" Had she any friends down here staying in the neighbourhood?"

" Not that I know of. Oh, I'm sure she hadn't."

" Now, Mr. Redfern, I want you to think very carefully. You knew Mrs. Marshall in London. You must be acquainted with various members of her circle. Is there any one you know of who could have had a grudge against her? Someone, for instance, whom you may have supplanted in her fancy?"

Patrick Redfern thought for some minutes. Then he shook his head.

" Honestly," he said. " I can't think of any one."

Colonel Weston drummed with his fingers on the table. He said at last:

" Well, that's that. We seem to be left with three possibilities. That of an unknown killer—some monomaniac —who happened to be in the neighbourhood—and that's a pretty tall order——"

Redfern said, interrupting:

" And yet surely, it's by far the most likely explanation."

Weston shook his head. He said:

" This isn't one of the ' lonely copse ' murders. This cove place was pretty inaccessible. Either the man would have to come up from the causeway past the hotel, over the top of the island and down by that ladder contraption, or else he came there by boat. Either way in unlikely for a casual killing."

Patrick Redfern said:

" You said there were three possibilities."

" Um—yes," said the Chief Constable. " That's to say,

there were two people on this island who had a motive for killing her. Her husband, for one, and your wife for another."

Redfern stared at him. He looked dumbfounded. He said: " My wife? Christine? D'you mean that *Christine* had anything to do with this?"

He got up and stood there stammering slightly in his incoherent haste to get the words out.

"You're mad—quite mad—Christine? Why, it's *impossible*. It's laughable!"

Weston said:

" All the same, Mr. Redfern, jealous is a very powerful motive. Women who are jealous lose control of themselves completely."

Redfern said earnestly.

" Not Christine. She's—oh she's not like that. She was unhappy, yes. But she's not the kind of person to—— Oh, there's no violence in her."

Hercule Poirot nodded thoughtfully. Violence. The same word that Linda Marshall had used. As before, he agreed with the sentiment.

"Besides," went on Redfern confidently. "It would be absurd. Arlena was twice as strong physically as Christine. I doubt if Christine could strangle a kitten—certainly not a strong wiry creature like Arlena. And then Christine could never have got down that ladder to the beach. She has no head for that sort of thing. And—oh, the whole thing is fantastic!"

Colonel Weston scratched his ear tentatively.

"Well," he said. " Put like that it doesn't seem likely. I grant you that. But motive's the first thing we've got to look for." He added: " Motive and opportunity."

4

When Redfern had left the room, the Chief Constable observed with a slight smile:

" Didn't think it necessary to tell the fellow his wife had got an alibi. Wanted to hear what he'd have to say to the idea. Shook him up a bit, didn't it?"

Hercule Poirot murmured:

" The arguments he advanced were quite as strong as any alibi."

" Yes. Oh! she didn't do it! She couldn't have done it— physically impossible as you said. Marshall *could* have done it—but apparently he didn't."

Inspector Colgate coughed. He said:

" Excuse me, sir, I've been thinking about that alibi. It's possible, you know, if he'd thought this thing out, that those lettters were got ready *beforehand*."

Weston said:

" That's a good idea. We must look into——"

He broke off as Christine Redfern entered the room.

She was, as always, calm and a little precise in manner. She was wearing a white tennis frock and a pale blue pullover. It accentuated her fair, rather anæmic prettiness. Yet, Hercule Poirot thought to himself, it was neither a silly face nor a weak one. It had plenty of resolution, courage and good sense. He nodded appreciatively.

Colonel Weston thought:

" Nice little woman. Bit wishy-washy, perhaps. A lot too good for that philandering young ass of a husband of hers. Oh well, the boy's young. Women usually make a fool of you once!"

He said:

" Sit down, Mrs. Redfern. We've got to go through a certain amount of routine, you see. Asking everybody for an account of their movements this morning. Just for our records."

Christine Redfern nodded.

She said in her quiet precise voice.

" Oh yes, I quite understand. Where do you want me to begin?"

Hercule Poirot said:

" As early as possible, Madame. What did you do when you first got up this morning?"

Christine said:

" Let me see. On my way down to breakfast I went into Linda Marshall's room and fixed up with her to go to Gull Cove this morning. We agreed to meet in the lounge at half-past ten."

Poirot asked:

" You did not bathe before breakfast, Madame?"

" No. I very. seldom do." She smiled. " I like the sea well warmed before I get into it. I'm rather a chilly person."

" But your husband bathes then?"

" Oh, yes. Nearly always."

" And Mrs. Marshall, she also?"

A change came over Christine's voice. It became cold and almost acrid.

She said:

" Oh no, Mrs. Marshall was the sort of person who never made an appearance before the middle of the morning."

With an air of confusion, Hercule Poirot said:

" Pardon, Madame, I interrupted you. You were saying that you went to Miss Linda Marshall's room. What time was that?"

" Let me see—half-past eight—no, a little later."

" And was Miss Marshall up then?"

" Oh yes, she had been out."

" Out?"

" Yes, she said she'd been bathing."

There was a faint—a very faint note of embarrassment in Christine's voice. It puzzled Hercule Poirot.

Weston said:

" And then?"

" Then I went down to breakfast."

" And after breakfast?"

" I went upstairs, collected my sketching box and sketching book and we started out."

" You and Miss Linda Marshall?"

" Yes."

" What time was that?"

" I think it was just on half-past ten."

" And what did you do?"

" We went to Gull Cove. You know, the cove on the east side of the island. We settled ourselves there. I did a sketch and Linda sunbathed."

" What time did you leave the cove?"

" At a quarter to twelve. I was playing tennis at twelve and had to change."

" You had your watch with you?"

" No, as a matter of fact I hadn't. I asked Linda the time."

" I see. And then?"

"I packed up my sketching things and went back to the hotel."

Poirot said:

"And Mademoiselle Linda?"

"Linda? Oh, Linda went into the sea."

Poirot said:

"Were you far from the sea where you were sitting?"

"Well, we were well above high-water mark. Just under the cliff—so that I could be a little in the shade and Linda in the sun."

Poirot said:

"Did Linda Marshall actually enter the sea before you left the beach?"

Christine frowned a little in the effort to remember. She said:

"Let me see. She ran down the beach—I fastened my box—— Yes, I heard her splashing in the waves as I was on the path up the cliff."

"You are quite sure of that, Madame? That she really entered the sea?"

"Oh yes."

She stared at him in surprise.

Colonel Weston also stared at him.

Then he said:

"Go on, Mrs. Redfern."

"I went back to the hotel, changed, and went to the tennis courts where I met the others."

"Who were?"

"Captain Marshall, Mr. Gardener and Miss Darnley. We played two sets. We were just going in again when the news came about—about Mrs. Marshall."

Hercule Poirot leant forward. He said:

"And what did you think, Madame, when you heard that news?"

"What did I think?"

Her face showed a faint distaste for the question.

"Yes."

Christine Redfern said slowly:

"It was—a horrible thing to happen."

"Ah, yes, your fastidiousness was revolted. I understand that. But what did it mean to *you*—personally?"

She gave him a quick look—a look of appeal. He responded to it. He said in a matter-of-fact voice.

"I am appealing to you, Madame, as a woman of intelligence with plenty of good sense and judgment. You had doubtless during your stay here formed an opinion of Mrs. Marshall, of the kind of woman she was?"

Christine said cautiously:

"I suppose one always does that more or less when one is staying in hotels."

"Certainly, it is the natural thing to do. So I ask you, Madame, were you really very surprised at the manner of her death?"

Christine said slowly:

"I think I see what you mean. No, I was not, perhaps, surprised. Shocked, yes. But she was the kind of woman——"

Poirot finished the sentence for her.

"She was the kind of woman to whom such a thing might happen . . . Yes, Madame, that is the truest and most significant thing that has been said in this room this morning. Laying all—er (he stressed it carefully) *personal* feeling aside, what did you really think of the late Mrs. Marshall?"

Christine Redfern said calmly:

"Is it really worth while going into all that now?"

"I think it might be, yes."

"Well, what shall I say?" Her fair skin was suddenly suffused with colour. The careful poise of her manner was relaxed. For a short space the natural raw woman looked out. "She's the kind of woman that to my mind is absolutely worthless! She did nothing to justify her existence. She had no mind—no brains. She thought of nothing but men and clothes and admiration. Useless, a parasite! She was attractive to men, I suppose—— Oh, of course she was. And she lived for that kind of life. And so, I suppose, I wasn't really surprised at her coming to a sticky end. She was the sort of woman who would be mixed up with everything sordid—blackmail—jealousy—violence—every kind of crude emotion. She—she appealed to the worst in people."

She stopped, panting a little. Her rather short top lip lifted itself in a kind of fastidious disgust. It occurred to Colonel Weston that you could not have found a more complete contrast to Arlena Stuart than Christine Redfern. It also occurred to him that if you were married to Christine Redfern, the atmosphere might be so rarefied that the Arlena Stuarts of this world would hold a particular attraction for you.

And then, immediately following on these thoughts, a single word out of the words she had spoken fastened on his attention with particular intensity.

He leaned forward and said:

" Mrs. Redfern, why, in speaking of her, did you mention the word *blackmail?* "

Chapter Seven

1

CHRISTINE stared at him, not seeming at once to take in what he meant She answered almost mechanically.

" I suppose—because she *was* being blackmailed. She was the sort of person who would be."

Colonel Weston said earnestly:

" But—do you know she was being blackmailed?"

A faint colour rose in the girl's cheeks. She said rather awkwardly:

" As a matter of fact I do happen to know it. I—I overheard something."

" Will you explain, Mrs. Redfern?"

Flushing still more, Christine Redfern said:

" I—I didn't mean to overhear. It was an accident. It was two—no, three nights ago. We were playing bridge." She turned towards Poirot. " You remember? My husband and I, M. Poirot and Miss Darnley. I was dummy. It was very stuffy in the card room, and I slipped out of the window for a breath of fresh air. I went down towards the beach and I suddenly heard voices. One—it was Arlena Marshall's—I knew it at once—said: ' It's no good pressing me. I can't get any more money now. My husband will suspect something.' And then a man's voice said: ' I'm not taking any excuses. You've got to cough up.' And then Arlena Marshall said: ' You blackmailing brute!' And the man said: ' Brute or not, you'll pay up, my lady.' "

Christine paused.

" I'd turned back and a minute after Arlena Marshall rushed past me. She looked—well, frightfully upset."

Weston said :

" And the man? Do you know who he was?"

Christine Redfern shook her head.

She said :

" He was keeping his voice low. I barely heard what he said."

" It didn't suggest the voice to you of any one you knew?"

She thought again, but once more shook her head. She said :

" No, I don't know. It was gruff and low. It—oh, it might have been anybody's."

Colonel Weston said :

" Thank you, Mrs. Redfern."

2

When the door had closed behind Christine Redfern Inspector Colgate said :

" Now we are getting somewhere!"

Weston said :

" You think so, eh?"

" Well, it's suggestive, sir, you can't get away from it. Somebody in this hotel was blackmailing the lady."

Poirot murmured :

" But it is not the wicked blackmailer who lies dead. It is the victim."

" That's a bit of a setback, I agree," said the Inspector. " Blackmailers aren't in the habit of bumping off their victims. But what it does give us is this, it suggests a reason for Mrs. Marshall's curious behaviour this morning. She'd got a rendezvous with this fellow who was blackmailing her, and she didn't want either her husband or Redfern to know about it."

" It certainly explains that point," agreed Poirot.

Inspector Colgate went on :

" And think of the place chosen. The very spot for the purpose. The lady goes off on her float. That's natural enough. It's what she does every day. She goes round to

Pixy Cove where no one ever goes in the morning and which will be a nice quiet place for an interview."

Poirot said:

" But yes, I too was struck by that point. It is as you say, an ideal spot for a *rendezvous*. It is deserted, it is only accessible from the land side by descending a vertical steel ladder which is not everybody's money, *bien entendu*. Moreover most of the beach is invisible from above because of the overhanging cliff. And it has another advantage. Mr. Redfern told me of that one day. There is a cave on it, the entrance to which is not easy to find but where any one could wait unseen."

Weston said:

" Of course, the Pixy's Cave—remember hearing about it."

Inspector Colgate said:

" Haven't heard it spoken of for years, though. We'd better have a look inside it. Never know, we might find a pointer of some kind."

Weston said:

" Yes, you're right, Colgate, we've got the solution to part one of the puzzle. *Why did Mrs. Marshall go to Pixy's Cove?* We want the other half of that solution, though. *Who did she go there to meet?* Presumably someone staying in this hotel. None of them fitted as a lover—but a blackmailer's a different proposition."

He drew the register towards him.

" Excluding the waiters, boots, etc., whom I don't think likely, we've got the following. The American—Gardener, Major Barry, Mr. Horace Blatt, and the Reverend Stephen Lane."

Inspector Colgate said:

" We can narrow it down a bit, sir. We might almost rule out the American, I think. He was on the beach all the morning. That's so, isn't it, M. Poirot?"

Poirot replied:

" He was absent for a short time when he fetched a skein of wool for his wife."

Colgate said:

" Oh well, we needn't count that."

Weston said:

" And what about the other three?"

"Major Barry went out at ten o'clock this morning. He returned at one-thirty. Mr. Lane was earlier still. He breakfasted at eight. Said he was going for a tramp. Mr. Blatt went off for a sail at nine-thirty same as he does most days. Neither of them are back yet."

"A sail, eh?" Colonel Weston's voice was thoughtful.

Inspector Colgate's voice was responsive. He said:

"Might fit in rather well, sir."

Weston said:

"Well, we'll have a word with this Major bloke— and let me see, who else is there? Rosamund Darnley. And there's the Brewster woman who found the body with Redfern. What's she like, Colgate?"

"Oh, a sensible party, sir. No nonsense about her."

"She didn't express any opinions on the death?"

The Inspector shook his head.

"I don't think she'll have anything more to tell us, sir, but we'll have to make sure. Then there are the Americans."

Colonel Weston nodded. He said: "Let's have 'em all in and get it over as soon as possible. Never know, might learn something. About the blackmailing stunt if about nothing else."

3

Mr. and Mrs. Gardener came into the presence of authority together.

Mrs. Gardener explained immediately.

"I hope you'll understand how it is, Colonel Weston (that is the name, I think?)." Reassured on this point she went on: "But this has been a very bad shock to me and Mr. Gardener is always very, very careful of my health——"

Mr. Gardener here interpolated:

"Mrs Gardener," he said, "is very sensitive."

"—— and he said to me, 'Why, Carrie,' he said, 'naturally I'm coming right along with you.' It's not that we haven't the highest admiration for British police methods because we have. I've been told that British police procedure is most refined and delicate, and I've never doubted it, and certainly when I once had a bracelet missing at the Savoy Hotel nothing could have been more lovely and sympathetic than the young

man who came to see me about it, and, of course, I
hadn't really lost the bracelet at all, but just mislaid it; that's
the worst of rushing about so much, it makes you kind
of forgetful where you put things——" Mrs. Gardener
paused, inhaled gently and started off again. "And what
I say is, and I know Mr. Gardener agrees with me, that
we're only too anxious to do anything to help the British police
in every way. So go right ahead and ask me anything at all
you want to know——"

Colonel Weston opened his mouth to comply with this
invitation, but had momentarily to postpone speech while
Mrs. Gardener went on.

"That's what I said, Odell, isn't it? And that's so, isn't it?"

"Yes, darling," said Mr. Gardener.

Colonel Weston spoke hastily.

"I understand, Mrs. Gardener, that you and your husband were on the beach all the morning?"

For once Mr. Gardener was able to get in first.

"That's so," he said.

"Why, certainly we were," said Mrs. Gardener. "And a
lovely peaceful morning it was, just like any other morning
if you get me, perhaps even more so, and not the slightest idea
in our minds of what was happening round the corner on
that lonely beach."

"Did you see Mrs. Marshall at all to-day?"

"We did not. And I said to Odell, why wherever can Mrs.
Marshall have got to this morning? I said. And first her
husband coming looking for her and then that good-looking
young man, Mr. Redfern, and so impatient he was, just
sitting there on the beach scowling at every one and everything. And I said to myself why, when he has that nice
pretty little wife of his own, must he go running after that
dreadful woman? Because that's just what I felt she was.
I always felt that about her, didn't I, Odell?"

"Yes, darling."

"However that nice Captain Marshall came to marry such
a woman I just cannot imagine and with that nice young
daughter growing up, and it's so important for girls to have
the right influence. Mrs. Marshall was not at all the right
person—no breeding at all—and I should say a very animal
nature. Now if Captain Marshall had had any sense he'd have
married Miss Darnley, who's a very very charming woman

and a very distinguished one. I must say I admire the way she's gone straight ahead and built up a first-class business as she has. It takes brains to do a thing like that—and you've only got to look at Rosamund Darnley to see she's just frantic with brains. She could plan and carry out any mortal thing she liked. I just admire that woman more than I can say. And I said to Mr. Gardener the other day that any one could see she was very much in love with Captain Marshall—crazy about him was what I said, didn't I, Odell?"

" Yes, darling."

" It seems they knew each other as children, and why now, who knows, it may all come right after all with that woman out of the way. I'm not a narrow-minded woman, Colonel Weston, and it isn't that I disapprove of the stage as such—why, quite a lot of my best friends are actresses—but I've said to Mr. Gardener all along that there was something evil about that woman. And you see, I've been proved right."

She paused triumphantly.

The lips of Hercule Poirot quivered in a little smile. His eyes met for a minute the shrewd grey eyes of Mr. Gardener.

Colonel Weston said rather desperately:

" Well, thank you, Mrs. Gardener. I suppose there's nothing that either of you has noticed since you've been here that might have a bearing upon the case?"

" Why no, I don't think so." Mr. Gardener spoke with a slow drawl. " Mrs. Marshall was around with young Redfern most of the time—but everybody can tell you that."

" What about her husband? Did he mind, do you think?"

Mr. Gardener said cautiously:

" Captain Marshall is a very reserved man."

Mrs. Gardener confirmed this by saying:

" Why, yes, he is a real Britisher!"

4

On the slightly apoplectic countenance of Major Barry various emotions seemed contending for mastery. He was endeavouring to look properly horrified but could not subdue a kind of shamefaced gusto.

He was saying in his hoarse, slightly wheezy voice:

" Glad to help you any way I can. 'Course I don't know

anythin' about it—nothin' at all. Not acquainted with the parties. But I've knocked about a bit in my time. Lived a lot in the East, you know. And I can tell you that after being in an Indian hill station what you don't know about human nature isn't worth knowin'."

He paused, took a breath and was off again.

" Matter of fact this business reminds me of a case in Simla. Fellow called Robinson, or was it Falconer? Anyway he was in the East Wilts, or was it the North Surreys? Can't remember now, and anyway it doesn't matter. Quiet chap, you know, great reader—mild as milk you'd have said. Went for his wife one evening in their bungalow. Got her by the throat. She'd been carryin' on with some feller or other and he'd got wise to it. By Jove, he nearly did for her! It was touch and go. Surprised us all! Didn't think he had it in him."

Hercule Poirot murmured:

" And you see there an analogy to the death of Mrs. Marshall?"

"Well, what I mean to say—strangled, you know. Same idea. Feller suddenly sees red!"

Poirot said:

" You think that Captain Marshall felt like that?"

"Oh, look here, I never said that." Major Barry's face went even redder. "Never said anything about Marshall. Thoroughly nice chap. Wouldn't say a word against him for the world."

Poirot murmured:-

" Ah, *pardon*, but you *did* refer to the natural reactions of a husband."

Major Barry said:

"Well, I mean to say, I should think she'd been pretty hot stuff. Eh? Got young Redfern on a string all right. And there were probably others before him. But the funny thing is, you know, that husbands are a dense lot. Amazin'. I've been surprised by it again and again. They see a feller sweet on their wife but they don't see that *she's* sweet on *him!* Remember a case like that in Poona. Very pretty woman. Jove, she led her husband a dance——"

Colonel Weston stirred a little restively. He said:

" Yes, yes, Major Barry. For the moment we've just got to establish the facts. You don't know of anything personally

—that you've seen or noticed that might help us in this case?"

" Well, really, Weston, I can't say I do. Saw her and young Redfern one afternoon on Gull Cove "—here he winked knowingly and gave a deep hoarse chuckle—" very pretty it was, too. But it's not èvidence of that kind you're wanting. Ha, ha!"

" You did not see Mrs. Marshall at all this morning?"

" Didn't see anybody this morning. Went over to St. Loo. Just my luck. Sort of place here where nothin' happens for months and when it does you miss it!"

The Major's voice held a ghoulish regret.

Colonel Weston prompted him.

" You went to St. Loo, you say?"

" Yes, wanted to do some telephonin'. No telephone here and that post-office place at Leathercombe Bay isn't very private."

" Were your telephone calls of a very private nature?"

The Major winked again cheerfully.

" Well, they were and they weren't. Wanted to get through to a pal of mine and get him to put somethin' on a horse. Couldn't get through to him, worse luck."

" Where did you telephone from?"

" Call box in the G.P.O. at St Loo. Then on the way back I got lost—these confounded lanes—twistin' and turnin' all over the place. Must have wasted an hour over that at least. Damned confusing part of the world. I only got back half an hour ago."

Colonel Weston said:

" Speak to any one or meet any one in St. Loo?"

Major Barry said with a chuckle:

" Wantin' me to prove an alibi? Can't think of anythin' useful. Saw about fifty thousand people in St. Loo—but that's not to say they'll remember seein' me."

The Chief Constable said:

" We have to ask these things, you know."

" Right you are. Call on me at any time. Glad to help you. Very fetchin' woman, the deceased. Like to help you catch the feller who did it. The Lonely Beach Murder—bet you that's what the papers will call it. Reminds me of the time——"

It was Inspector Colgate who firmly nipped this latest reminiscence in the bud and manœuvred the garrulous Major out of the door.

Coming back he said:

"Difficult to check up on anything in St. Loo. It's the middle of the holiday season."

The Chief Constable said:

"Yes, we can't take him off the list. Not that I seriously believe he's implicated. Dozens of old bores like him going about. Remember one or two of them in my army days. Still—he's a possibility. I leave all that to you, Colgate. Check what time he took the car out—petrol—all that. It's humanly possible that he parked the car somewhere in a lonely spot, walked back here and went to the cove. But it doesn't seem feasible to me. He'd have run too much risk of being seen."

Colgate nodded.

He said:

"Of course there are a good many charabancs here to-day. Fine day. They start arriving round about half-past eleven. High tide was at seven. Low tide would be about one o'clock. People would be spread out over the sands and the causeway."

Weston said:

"Yes. But he'd have to come up from the causeway past the hotel."

"Not right past it. He could branch off on the path that leads up over the top of the island."

Weston said doubtfully:

"I'm not saying that he mightn't have done it without being seen. Practically all the hotel guests were on the bathing beach except for Mrs. Redfern and the Marshall girl who were down in Gull Cove, and the beginning of that path would only be overlooked by a few rooms of the hotel and there are plenty of chances against any one looking out of those windows just at that moment. For the matter of that, I dare say it's possible for a man to walk up to the hotel, through the lounge and out again without any one happening to see him. But what I say is, he couldn't *count* on no one seeing him."

Colgate said:

"He could have gone round to the cove by boat."

Weston nodded. He said:

"That's much sounder. If he'd had a boat handy in one of the coves nearby, he could have left the car, rowed or sailed to Pixy's Cove, done the murder, rowed back, picked up the car and arrived back with this tale about having been to St. Loo and lost his way—a story that he'd know would be pretty hard to disprove."

" You're right, sir."

The Chief Constable said:

" Well, I leave it to you, Colgate. Comb the neighbourhood thoroughly. You know what to do. We'd better see Miss Brewster now."

5

Emily Brewster was not able to add anything of material value to what they already knew.

Weston said after she had repeated her story:

" And there's nothing you know of that could help us in any way?"

Emily Brewster said shortly:

" Afraid not It's a distressing business. However, I expect you'll soon get to the bottom of it."

Weston said:

" I hope so, I'm sure."

Emily Brewster said dryly:

" Ought not to be difficult."

" Now what do you mean by that, Miss Brewster?"

" Sorry Wasn't attempting to teach you your business. All I meant was that with a woman of that kind it ought to be easy enough."

Hercule Poirot murmured:

" That is your opinion?"

Emily Brewster snapped out:

" Of course. *De mortuis nil nisi bonum* and all that, but you can't get away from *facts*. That woman was a bad lot through and through. You've only got to hunt round a bit in her unsavoury past."

Hercule Poirot said gently:

" You did not like her?"

" I know a bit too much about her." In answer to the inquiring looks she went on: " My first cousin married one of the Erskines. You've probably heard that that woman induced old Sir Robert when he was in his dotage to leave most of his fortune to her away from his own family."

Colonel Weston said:

" And the family—er—resented that?"

" Naturally. His association with her was a scandal anyway, and on top of that, to leave her a sum like fifty thousand pounds shows just the kind of woman she was. I dare say I sound hard, but in my opinion the Arlena Stuarts of this world deserve very little sympathy. I know of something else too—a young fellow who lost his head about her completely—he'd always been a bit wild, naturally his association with her pushed him over the edge. He did something rather fishy with some shares—solely to get money to spend on her—and only just managed to escape prosecution. That woman contaminated every one she met. Look at the way she was ruining young Redfern. No, I'm afraid I can't have any regret for her death—though of course it would have been better if she'd drowned herself, or fallen over a cliff. Strangling is rather unpleasant."

" And you think the murderer was someone out of her past?"

" Yes, I do."

" Someone who came from the mainland with no one seeing him?"

" Why should any one see him? We were all on the beach. I gather the Marshall child and Christine Redfern were down on Gull Cove out of the way. Captain Marshall was in his room in the hotel. Then who on earth was there to see him except possibly Miss Darnley."

" Where was Miss Darnley?"

" Sitting up on the cutting at the top of the cliff. Sunny Ledge it's called. We saw her there, Mr. Redfern and I, when we were rowing round the island."

Colonel Weston said:

" You may be right, Miss Brewster."

Emily Brewster said positively:

" I'm sure I'm right. When a woman's neither more nor less than a nasty mess, then she herself will provide the best possible clue. Don't you agree with me, M. Poirot?"

Hercule Poirot looked up. His eyes met her confident grey ones. He said:

" Oh, yes—I agree with that which you have just this minute said. Arlena Marshall herself is the best, the only clue, to her own death."

Miss Brewster said sharply:

" Well, then!"

She stood there, an erect sturdy figure, her cool self-confident glance going from one man to the other.

Colonel Weston said:

" You may be sure, Miss Brewster, that any clue there may be in Mrs. Marshall's past life will not be overlooked."

Emily Brewster went out.

6

Inspector Colgate shifted his position at the table. He said in a thoughtful voice:

" She's a determined one, she is. And she'd got her knife into the dead lady, proper, she had."

He stopped a minute and said reflectively:

" It's a pity in a way that she's got a cast-iron alibi for the whole morning. Did you notice her hands, sir? As big as a man's. And she's a hefty woman—as strong and stronger than many a man, I'd say . ."

He paused again His glance at Poirot was almost pleading.

" And you say she never left the beach this morning, M. Poirot?"

Slowly Poirot shook his head. He said:

" My dear Inspector, she came down to the beach before Mrs. Marshall could have reached Pixy's Cove and she was within my sight until she set off with Mr. Redfern in the boat."

Inspector Colgate said gloomily:

" Then that washes her out."

He seemed upset about it.

7

As always, Hercule Poirot felt a keen sense of pleasure at the sight of Rosamund Darnley.

Even to a bare police inquiry into the ugly facts of murder she brought a distinction of her own.

She sat down opposite Colonel Weston and turned a grave and intelligent face to him.

She said:

"You want my name and address? Rosamund Anne Darnley. I carry on a dressmaking business under the name of Rose Mond Ltd. at 622 Brook Street."

"Thank you, Miss Darnley. Now can you tell us anything that may help us?"

"I don't really think I can."

"Your own movements——"

"I had breakfast about nine-thirty. Then I went up to my room and collected some books and my sunshade and went out to Sunny Ledge. That must have been about twenty-five past ten. I came back to the hotel about ten minutes to twelve, went up and got my tennis racquet and went out to the tennis courts, where I played tennis until lunch-time."

"You were in the cliff recess, called by the hotel Sunny Ledge, from about half-past ten until ten minutes to twelve?"

"Yes."

"Did you see Mrs. Marshall at all this morning?"

"No."

"Did you see her from the cliff as she paddled her float round to Pixy's Cove?"

"No, she must have gone by before I got there."

"Did you notice any one on a float or in a boat at all this morning?"

"No, I don't think I did. You see, I was reading. Of course I looked up from my book from time to time, but as it happened the sea was quite bare each time I did so."

"You didn't even notice Mr. Redfern and Miss Brewster when they went round?"

"No."

"You were, I think, acquainted with Mrs. Marshall?"

"Captain Marshall is an old family friend. His family and

mine lived next door to each other. I had not seen him, however, for a good many years—it must be something like twelve years."

" And Mrs. Marshall?"

" I'd never exchanged half a dozen words with her until I met her here."

" Were Captain and Mrs. Marshall, as far as you knew, on good terms with each other?"

" On perfectly good terms, I should say."

" Was Captain Marshall very devoted to his wife?"

Rosamund said:

" He may have been. I can't really tell you anything about that. Captain Marshall is rather old-fashioned—he hasn't got the modern habit of shouting matrimonial woes upon the housetop."

" Did you like Mrs. Marshall, Miss Darnley?"

" No."

The monosyllable came quietly and evenly. It sounded what it was—a simple statement of fact."

" Why was that?"

A half smile came to Rosamund's lips. She said:

" Surely you've discovered that Arlena Marshall was not popular with her own sex? She was bored to death with women and showed it. Nevertheless I should like to have had the dressing of her. She had a great gift for clothes. Her clothes were always just right and she wore them well. I should like to have had her as a client."

" She spent a good deal on clothes?"

" She must have done. But then she had money of her own and of course Captain Marshall is quite well off."

" Did you ever hear or did it ever occur to you that Mrs. Marshall was being blackmailed, Miss Darnley?"

A look of intense astonishment came over Rosamund Darnley's expressive face.

She said:

" Blackmailed? Arlena?"

" The idea seems to surprise you."

" Well, yes, it does rather. It seems so incongruous."

" But surely it is possible?"

" Everything's possible, isn't it? The world soon teaches one that. But I wondered what any one could blackmail Arlena about?"

"There are certain things, I suppose, that Mrs. Marshall might be anxious should not come to her husband's ears?"

"We-ll, yes."

She explained the doubt in her voice by saying with a half smile:

"I sound sceptical, but then, you see, Arlena was rather notorious in her conduct. She never made much of a pose of respectability."

"You think, then, that her husband was aware of her—intimacies with other people?"

There was a pause. Rosamund was frowning. She spoke at last in a slow, reluctant voice. She said:

"You know, I don't really know what to think. I've always assumed that Kenneth Marshall accepted his wife, quite frankly, for what she was. That he had no illusions about her. But it may not be so."

"He may have believed in her absolutely?"

Rosamund said with semi-exasperation:

"Men are such fools. And Kenneth Marshall is unworldly under his sophisticated manner. He *may* have believed in her blindly He may have thought she was just—admired."

"And you know of no one—that is, you have heard of no one who was likely to have had a grudge against Mrs. Marshall?"

Rosamund Darnley smiled. She said:

"Only resentful wives. And I presume, since she was strangled, that it was a man who killed her."

"Yes."

Rosamund said thoughtfully:

"No, I can't think of any one. But then I probably shouldn't know. You'll have to ask someone in her own intimate set."

"Thank you, Miss Darnley."

Rosamund turned a little in her chair. She said:

"Hasn't M. Poirot any questions to ask?"

Her faintly ironic smile flashed out at him.

Hercule Poirot smiled and shook his head.

He said:

"I can think of nothing."

Rosamund Darnley got up and went out.

Chapter Eight

1

THEY were standing in the bedroom that had been Arlena Marshall's.

Two big bay windows gave on to a balcony that overlooked the bathing beach and the sea beyond. Sunshine poured into the room, flashing over the bewildering array of bottles and jars on Arlena's dressing-table.

Here there was every kind of cosmetic and unguent known to beauty parlours. Amongst this panoply of woman's affairs three men moved purposefully. Inspector Colgate went about shutting and opening drawers.

Presently he gave a grunt. He had come upon a packet of folded letters. He and Weston ran through them together.

Hercule Poirot had moved to the wardrobe. He opened the door of the hanging cupboard and looked at the multiplicity of gowns and sports suits that hung there. He opened the other side. Foamy lingerie lay in piles. On a wide shelf were hats. Two more beach cardboard hats in lacquer red and pale yellow—a big Hawaiian straw hat—another of drooping dark-blue linen and three or four little absurdities for which, no doubt, several guineas had been paid apiece—a kind of beret in dark blue—a tuft, no more, of black velvet —a pale grey turban.

Hercule Poirot stood scanning them—a faintly indulgent smile came to his lips. He murmured:

" *Les femmes!* "

Colonel Weston was refolding the letters.

" Three from young Redfern," he said. " Damned young ass. He'll learn not to write letters to women in a few more years. Women always keep letters and then swear they've burnt them. There's one other letter here. Same line of country."

He held it out and Poirot took it.

" Darling Arlena,—God, I feel blue. To be going out to China—and perhaps not seeing you again for years and years.

I didn't know any man could go on feeling crazy about a woman like I feel about you. Thanks for the cheque. They won't prosecute now. It was a near shave, though, and all because I wanted to make big money for you. Can you forgive me? I wanted to set diamonds in your ears—your lovely ears—and clasp great milk-white pearls round your throat, only they say pearls are no good nowadays. A fabulous emerald. then? Yes, that's the thing. A great emerald, cool and green and full of hidden fire. Don't forget me—but you won't, I know. You're mine—always.

" Good-bye—good-bye—good-bye.

" J.N."

Inspector Colgate said:

" Might be worth while to find out if J.N. really did go to China Otherwise—well, he might be the person we're looking for. Crazy about the woman, idealising her, suddenly finding out he'd been played for a sucker. It sounds to me as though this is the boy Miss Brewster mentioned. Yes, I think this might be useful."

Hercule Poirot nodded He said: " Yes, that letter is important I find it very important."

He turned round and stared at the room—at the bottles on the dressing-table—at the open wardrobe and at a big Pierrot doll that lolled insolently on the bed.

They went into Kenneth Marshall's room.

It was next door to his wife's but with no communicating door and no balcony It faced the same way and had two windows, but it was much smaller. Between the two windows a gilt mirror hung on the wall. In the corner beyond the right-hand window was the dressing-table. On it were two ivory brushes, a clothes brush and a bottle of hair lotion. In the corner by the left-hand window was a writing-table An open typewriter stood on it and papers were ranged in a stack beside it.

Colgate went through them rapidly.

He said:

" All seems straightforward enough. Ah, here's the letter he mentioned this morning. Dated the 24th—that's yesterday. And here's the envelope postmarked Leathercombe Bay this morning. Seems all square. Now we'll have an idea if he could have prepared that answer of his beforehand.

He sat down.

Colonel Weston said:

"We'll leave you to it, for a moment. We'll just glance through the rest of the rooms. Everyone's been kept out of this corridor until now, and they're getting a bit restive about it."

They went next into Linda Marshall's room. It faced east, looking out over the rocks down to the sea below.

Weston gave a glance round. He murmured:

"Don't suppose there's anything to see here. But it's possible Marshall might have put something in his daughter's room that he didn't want us to find. Not likely, though. It isn't as though there had been a weapon or anything to get rid of."

He went out again.

Hercule Poirot stayed behind. He found something that interested him in the grate. Something had been burnt there recently. He knelt down, working patiently. He laid out his finds on a sheet of paper. A large irregular blob of candle grease—some fragments of green paper or cardboard, possibly a pull-off calendar for with it was an unburnt fragment bearing a large figure 5 and a scrap of printing . . . *noble deeds* . . . There was also an ordinary pin and some burnt animal matter which might have been hair.

Poirot arranged them neatly in a row and stared at them.

He murmured:

"*Do noble deeds, not dream them all day long. C'est possible* But what is one to make of this collection? *C'est fantastique!*"

And then he picked up the pin and his eyes grew sharp and green.

He murmured:

"*Pour l'amour de Dieu!* Is it possible?"

Hercule Poirot got up from where he had been kneeling by the grate.

Slowly he looked round the room and this time there was an entirely new expression on his face. It was grave and almost stern.

To the left of the mantelpiece there were some shelves with a row of books. Hercule Poirot looked thoughtfully along the titles.

A Bible, a battered copy of Shakespeare's plays, *The Marriage of William Ashe,* by Mrs. Humphry Ward. *The Young Stepmother,* by Charlotte Yonge. *The Shropshire Lad.* Eliot's *Murder in the Cathedral.* Bernard Shaw's *St. Joan.* *Gone with the Wind,* by Margaret Mitchell. *The Burning Court,* by Dickson Carr.

Poirot took out two books, *The Young Stepmother* and *William Ashe,* and glanced inside at the blurred stamp affixed to the title page. As he was about to replace them, his eye caught sight of a book that had been shoved behind the other books. It was a small dumpy volume bound in brown calf.

He took it out and opened it. Very slowly he nodded his head

He murmured:

"*So I was right.* . . . Yes, I was right. But for the other— is that possible too? No, it is not possible, unless . . ."

He stayed there, motionless. stroking his moustaches whilst his mind ranged busily over the problem.

He said again, softly:

"*Unless——?*"

2

Colonel Weston looked in at the door.

"Hullo, Poirot, still there?"

"I arrive. I arrive," cried Poirot.

He hurried out into the corridor.

The room next to Linda's was that of the Redferns.

Poirot looked into it, noting automatically the trace of two different individualities—a neatness and tidiness which he associated with Christine, and a picturesque disorder which was characteristic of Patrick. Apart from these sidelights on personality the room did not interest him.

Next to it again was Rosamund Darnley's room, and here he lingered for a moment in the sheer pleasure of the owner's personality.

He noted the few books that lay on the table next to the bed, the expensive simplicity of the toilet set on the dressing-table. And there came gently to his nostrils the elusive expensive perfume that Rosamund Darnley used.

Next to Rosamund Darnley's room at the northern end of the corridor was an open window leading to a balcony from which an outside stair led down to the rocks below.

Weston said:

"That's the way people go down to bathe before breakfast —that is, if they bathe off the rocks as most of them do."

Interest came into Hercule Poirot's eyes. He stepped outside and looked down.

Below, a path led to steps cut zigzag leading down the rocks to the sea. There was also a path that led round the hotel to the left. He said:

"One could go down these stairs, go to the left round the hotel and join the main path up from the causeway."

Weston nodded. He amplified Poirot's statement.

"One could go right across the island without going through the hotel at all." He added: "But one might still be seen from a window."

"What window?"

"Two of the public bathrooms look out that way—north— and the staff bathroom, and the cloakrooms on the ground floor. Also the billiard room."

Poirot nodded. He said:

"And all the former have frosted glass windows, and one does not play billiards on a fine morning."

"Exactly."

Weston paused and said:

"If he did it, that's the way he went."

"You mean Captain Marshall?"

"Yes. Blackmail, or no blackmail, I still feel it points to him. And his manner—well, his manner is unfortunate."

Hercule Poirot said dryly:

"Perhaps—but a manner does not make a murderer!"

Weston said:

"Then you think he's out of it?"

Poirot shook his head. He said:

"No, I would not say that."

Weston said:

"We'll see what Colgate can make out of the typewriting alibi. In the meantime I've got the chambermaid of this floor waiting to be interviewed. A good deal may depend on her evidence."

The chambermaid was a woman of thirty, brisk, efficient and intelligent. Her answers came readily.

Captain Marshall had come up to his room not long after ten-thirty. She was then finishing the room. He had asked her to be as quick as possible. She had not seen him come back but she had heard the sound of the typewriter a little later. She put it at about five minutes to eleven. She was then in Mr. and Mrs. Redfern's room. After she had done that she moved on to Miss Darnley's room at the end of the corridor. She could not hear the typewriter from there. She went to Miss Darnley's room, as near as she could say, at just after eleven o'clock. She remembered hearing Leathercombe Church strike the hour as she went in. At a quarter-past eleven she had gone downstairs for her eleven o'clock cup of tea and " snack." Afterwards she had gone to do the rooms in the other wing of the hotel. In answer to the Chief Constable's question she explained that she had done the rooms in this corridor in the following order:

Miss Linda Marshall's, the two public bathrooms, Mrs. Marshall's room and private bath, Captain Marshall's room. Mr. and Mrs. Redfern's room and private bath, Miss Darnley's room and private bath. Captain Marshall's and Miss Marshall's rooms had no adjoining bathrooms.

During the time she was in Miss Darnley's room and bath-room she had not heard any one pass the door or go out by the staircase to the rocks, but it was quite likely she wouldn't have heard if any one went quietly.

Weston then directed his questions to the subject of Mrs. Marshall.

No, Mrs. Marshall wasn't one for rising early as a rule. She, Gladys Narracott, had been surprised to find the door open and Mrs. Marshall gone down at just after ten. Something quite unusual, that was.

" Did Mrs. Marshall always have her breakfast in bed?"

" Oh yes, sir, always. Not very much of it either. Just tea and orange juice and one piece of toast. Slimming like so many ladies."

No, she hadn't noticed anything unusual in Mrs. Marshall's manner that morning. She'd seemed quite as usual.

Hercule Poirot murmured:

" What did you think of Mrs. Marshall, Mademoiselle?"

Gladys Narracott stared at him. She said:

" Well, that's hardly for me to say, is it, sir?"

" But yes, it is for you to say. We are anxious—very anxious—to hear your impression."

Gladys gave a slightly uneasy glance towards the Chief Constable, who endeavoured to make his face sympathetic and approving, though actually he felt slightly embarrassed by his foreign colleague's methods of approach. He said:

" Er—yes certainly. Go ahead."

For the first time Gladys Narracott's brisk efficiency deserted her. Her fingers fumbled with her print dress. She said:

" Well, Mrs. Marshall—she wasn't exactly a lady, as you might say. What I mean is she was more like an actress."

Colonel Weston said:

" She was an actress."

" Yes. sir, that's what I'm saying. She just went on exactly as she felt like it. She didn't—well, she didn't trouble to be polite if she wasn't feeling polite. And she'd be all smiles one minute and then, if she couldn't find something or the bell wasn't answered at once or her laundry wasn't back, well, be downright rude and nasty about it. None of us you might say *liked* her. But her clothes were beautiful, and, of course, she was a very handsome lady, so it was only natural she should be admired."

Colonel Weston said:

" I am sorry to have to ask you what I am going to ask you, but it is a very vital matter. Can you tell me how things were between her and her husband?"

Gladys Narracott hesitated a minute.

She said:

" You don't—it wasn't—you don't think as *he* did it?"

Hercule Poirot said quickly:

" Do you?"

" Oh! I wouldn't like to think so. He's such a nice gentleman, Captain Marshall. He couldn't do a thing like that—I'm sure he couldn't."

" But you are *not* very sure—I hear it in your voice."

Gladys Narracott said reluctantly:

" You do read such things in the papers! When there's jealousy. If there's been goings on—and, of course, every one's been talking about it—about her and Mr. Redfern,

I mean. And Mrs. Redfern such a nice quiet lady! It does seem a shame! And Mr. Redfern's a nice gentleman too, but it seems men can't help themselves when it's a lady like Mrs. Marshall—one who's used to having her own way. Wives have to put up with a lot, I'm sure." She sighed and paused. "But if Captain Marshall found out about it——"

Colonel Weston said sharply:

"Well?"

Gladys Narracott said slowly:

"I did think sometimes that Mrs. Marshall was frightened of her husband knowing."

"What makes you say that?"

"It wasn't anything definite, sir. It was only I felt—that sometimes she was—afraid of him. He was a very quiet gentleman but he wasn't—he wasn't *easy*."

Weston said:

"But you've nothing definite to go on? Nothing either of them ever said to each other."

Slowly Gladys Narracott shook her head.

Weston sighed. He went on.

"Now, as to letters received by Mrs. Marshall this morning. Can you tell us anything about those?"

"There were about six or seven, sir. I couldn't say exactly."

"Did you take them up to her?"

"Yes, sir. I got them from the office as usual and put them on her breakfast tray."

"Do you remember anything about the look of them?"

The girl shook her head.

"They were just ordinary-looking letters. Some of them were bills and circulars, I think, because they were torn up on the tray."

"What happened to them?"

"They went into the dustbin, sir. One of the police gentlemen is going through that now."

Weston nodded.

"And the contents of the waste-paper baskets, where are they?"

"They'll be in the dustbin too."

Weston said: "H'm—well, I think that is all at present." He looked inquiringly at Poirot.

Poirot leaned forward.

"When you did Miss Linda Marshall's room this morning, did you do the fireplace?"

"There wasn't anything to do, sir. There had been no fire lit."

"And there was nothing in the fireplace itself?"

"No sir, it was perfectly all right."

"What time did you do her room?"

"About a quarter-past nine, sir, when she'd gone down to breakfast."

"Did she come up to her room after breakfast, do you know?"

"Yes, sir. She came up about a quarter to ten."

"Did she stay in her room?"

"I think so, sir. She came out, hurrying rather, just before half-past ten."

"You didn't go into her room again?"

"No. sir. I had finished with it."

Poirot nodded. He said.

"There is another thing I want to know. What people bathed before breakfast this morning?"

"I couldn't say about the other wing and the floor above. Only about this one."

"That is all I want to know."

"Well, sir, Captain Marshall and Mr. Redfern were the only ones this morning, I think. They always go down for an early dip."

"Did you see them?"

"No, sir, but their wet bathing things were hanging over the balcony rail as usual."

"Miss Linda Marshall did not bathe this morning?"

"No, sir. All her bathing dresses were quite dry."

"Ah," said Poirot. "That is what I wanted to know."

Gladys Narracott volunteered:

"She does most mornings, sir."

"And the other three, Miss Darnley, Mrs. Redfern and Mrs. Marshall?"

"Mrs. Marshall never, sir. Miss Darnley has once or twice, I think. Mrs. Redfern doesn't often bathe before breakfast —only when it's very hot, but she didn't this morning."

Again Poirot nodded. Then he asked:

"I wonder if you have noticed whether a bottle is missing from any of the rooms you look after in this wing?"

" A bottle, sir? What kind of a bottle?"

" Unfortunately I do not know. But have you noticed—or would you be likely to notice—if one had gone?"

Gladys said frankly:

" I shouldn't from Mrs. Marshall's room, sir, and that's a fact. She has ever so many."

" And the other rooms?"

" Well, I'm not sure about Miss Darnley. She has a good many creams and lotions. But from the other rooms, yes, I would, sir. I mean if I were to look special. If I were noticing, so to speak."

" But you haven't actually noticed?"

" No, because I wasn't looking special, as I say."

" Perhaps you would go and look now, then."

" Certainly, sir."

She left the room, her print dress rustling. Weston looked at Poirot. He said: " What's all this?"

Poirot murmured:

" My orderly mind, that is vexed by trifles! Miss Brewster, this morning, was bathing off the rocks before breakfast, and she says that a bottle was thrown from above and nearly hit her. *Eh bien,* I want to know who threw that bottle and why?"

" My dear man, any one may have chucked a bottle away."

" Not at all. To begin with, it could only have been thrown from a window on the east side of the hotel—that is, one of the windows of the rooms we have just examined. Now I ask you, if you have an empty bottle on your dressing-table or in your bathroom what do you do with it? I will tell you, you drop it into the waste-paper basket. You do not take the trouble to go out on your balcony and hurl it into the sea! For one thing you might hit someone, for another it would be too much trouble. No, you would only do that *if you did not want any one to see that particular bottle.*"

Weston stared at him.

Weston said:

" I know that Chief Inspector Japp, whom I met over a case not long ago, always says you have a damned tortuous mind. You're not going to tell me now that Arlena Marshall wasn't strangled at all, but poisoned out of some mysterious bottle with a mysterious drug?"

" No, no, I do not think there was poison in that bottle."

" Then what was there?"

" I do not know at all. That's why I am interested."

Gladys Narracott came back. She was a little breathless.
She said:

" I'm sorry, sir, but I can't find anything missing. I'm sure
there's nothing gone from Captain Marshall's room, or Miss
Linda Marshall's room, or Mr. and Mrs. Redfern's room, and
I'm pretty sure there's nothing gone from Miss Darnley's
either. But I couldn't say about Mrs. Marshall's. As I say,
she's got such a lot."

Poirot shrugged his shoulders.

He said:

" No matter. We will leave it."

Gladys Narracott said:

" Is there anything more, sir?"

She looked from one to the other of them.

Weston said:

" Don't think so. Thank you."

Poirot said:

" I thank you, no. You are sure, are you not, that there
is nothing—nothing at all, that you have forgotten to tell us?"

" About Mrs. Marshall, sir?"

" About anything at all. Anything unusual, out of the way,
unexplained, slightly peculiar, rather curious—*enfin,* something that has made you say to yourself or to one of your
colleagues: ' That's funny!'?"

Gladys said doubtfully:

" Well, not the sort of thing that you would mean, sir?"

Hercule Poirot said:

" Never mind what I mean. You do not know what I
mean. It is true, then, that you have said to yourself or
to a colleague to-day, ' that is funny!'?"

He brought out the three words with ironic detachment.

Gladys said:

" It was nothing really. Just a bath being run. And I
did pass the remark to Elsie, downstairs, that it was funny
somebody having a bath round about twelve o'clock."

" Whose bath, who had a bath?"

" That I couldn't say, sir. We heard it going down the
waste from this wing, that's all, and that's when I said what
I did to Elsie."

" You're sure it was a bath? Not one of the hand-basins?"

" Oh! quite sure, sir. You can't mistake bath-water running away."

Poirot displaying no further desire to keep her, Gladys Narracott was permitted to depart.

Weston said:

" You don't think this bath question is important, do you, Poirot? I mean, there's no point to it. No bloodstains or anything like that to wash off. That's the——" He hesitated.

Poirot cut in:

" That, you would say, is the advantage of strangulation! No bloodstains, no weapon—nothing to get rid of or conceal! Nothing is needed but physical strength—*and the soul of a killer!*"

His voice was so fierce, so charged with feeling, that Weston recoiled a little.

Hercule Poirot smiled at him apologetically.

" No one," he said, " the bath is probably of no importance. Any one may have had a bath. Mrs. Redfern before she went to play tennis, Captain Marshall, Miss Darnley. As I say, any one. There is nothing in that."

A police constable knocked at the door, and put in his head.

" It's Miss Darnley, sir. She says she'd like to see you again for a minute. There's something she forgot to tell you, she says."

Weston said:

" We're coming down—now."

3

The first person they saw was Colgate. His face was gloomy.

" Just a minute, sir."

Weston and Poirot followed him into Mrs. Castle's office.

Colgate said:

" I've been checking-up with Heald on this type-writing business. Not a doubt of it, it couldn't be done under an hour. Longer, if you had to stop and think here and there. That seems to me pretty well to settle it. And look at this letter."

He held it out.

" *My dear Marshall—Sorry to worry you on your holiday but an entirely unforseen situation has arisen over the Burley and Tender contracts. . . .*"

" Etcetera, etcetera," said Colgate. " Dated the 24th—that's yesterday. Envelope postmarked yesterday evening E.C.1. and Leathercombe Bay this morning. Same typewriter used on envelope and in letter. And by the contents it was clearly impossible for Marshall to prepare his answer beforehand. The figures arise out of the ones in the letter—the whole thing is quite intricate."

" H'm," said Weston gloomily. " That seems to let Marshall out. We'll have to look elsewhere." He added: " I've got to see Miss Darnley again. She's waiting now."

Rosamund came in crisply. Her smile held an apologetic *nuance.*

She said:

" I'm frightfully sorry. Probably it isn't worth bothering about. But one does forget things so."

" Yes, Miss Darnley?"

The Chief Constable indicated a chair.

She shook her shapely black head.

" Oh, it isn't worth sitting down. It's simply this. I told you that I spent the morning lying out on Sunny Ledge. That isn't quite accurate. I forgot that once during the morning I went back to the hotel and out again."

" What time was that, Miss Darnley?"

" It must have been about a quarter-past eleven."

" You went back to the hotel, you said?"

" Yes, I'd forgotten my glare glasses. At first I thought I wouldn't bother and then my eyes got tired and I decided to go in and get them."

" You went straight to your room and out again?"

" Yes. At least, as a matter of fact, I just looked in on Ken —Captain Marshall. I heard his machine going and I thought it was so stupid of him to stay indoors typing on such a lovely day. I thought I'd tell him to come out."

" And what did Captain Marshall say?"

Rosamund smiled rather shamefacedly.

" Well, when I opened the door he was typing so vigorously, **and** frowning and looking so concentrated, that just went **away** quietly. I don't think he even saw me come in."

" And that was—at what time, Miss Darnley?"

" Just about twenty-past eleven. I noticed the clock in the hall as I went out again."

4

" And that puts the lid on it finally," said Inspector Colgate. " The chambermaid heard him typing up till five minutes to eleven. Miss Darnley saw him at twenty minutes past, and the woman was dead at a quarter to twelve. He says he spent that hour typing in his room, and it seems quite clear that he *was* typing in his room. That washes Captain Marshall right out."

He stopped, then looking at Poirot with some curiosity, he asked:

" M. Poirot's looking very serious over something."

Poirot said thoughtfully:

" I was wondering why Miss Darnley suddenly volunteered this extra evidence."

Inspector Colgate cocked his head alertly.

" Think there's something fishy about it? That it isn't just a question of ' forgetting '?"

He considered for a minute or two, then he said slowly:

" Look here, sir, let's look at it this way. Supposing Miss Darnley wasn't on Sunny Ledge this morning as she says. That story's a lie. Now suppose that *after* telling us her story, she finds that somebody saw her somewhere else or alternatively that someone went to the Ledge and didn't find her there. Then she thinks up this story quick and comes and tells it to us to account for her absence. You'll notice that she was careful to say Captain Marshall didn't *see* her when she looked into his room."

Poirot murmured:

" Yes, I noticed that."

Weston said incredulously:

" Are you suggesting that Miss Darnley's mixed up in this? Nonsense, seems absurd to me. Why should she be?"

Inspector Colgate coughed.

He said:

" You'll remember what the American lady, Mrs. Gardener,

said. She sort of hinted that Miss Darnley was sweet on Captain Marshall. There'd be a motive there, sir."

Weston said impatiently:

" Arlena Marshall wasn't killed by a woman. It's a man we've got to look for. We've got to stick to the men in the case."

Inspector Colgate sighed. He said:

" Yes, that's true, sir. We always come back to that, don't we?"

Weston went on:

" Better put a constable on to timing one or two things. From the hotel across the island to the top of the ladder. Let him do it running and walking. Same thing with the ladder itself. And somebody had better check the time it takes to go on a float from the bathing beach to the cove."

Inspector Colgate nodded.

" I'll attend to all that, sir," he said confidently.

The Chief Constable said:

" Think I'll go along to the cove now. See if Phillips has found anything. Then there's that Pixy's Cave we've been hearing about. Ought to see if there are any traces of a man waiting in there. Eh, Poirot? What do you think?"

" By all means. It is a possibility."

Weston said:

" If somebody from outside had nipped over to the island that would be a good hiding-place—if he knew about it. I suppose the locals know?"

Colgate said:

" Don't believe the younger generation would. You see, ever since this hotel was started the coves have been private property. Fishermen don't go there, or picnic parties. And the hotel people aren't local. Mrs. Castle's a Londoner."

Weston said:

" We might take Redfern with us. He told us about it. What about you, M. Poirot?"

Hercule Poirot hesitated. He said, his foreign intonation very pronounced:

" Me, I am like Miss Brewster and Mrs. Redfern, I do not like to descend perpendicular ladders."

Weston said: " You can go round by boat."

Again Hercule Poirot sighed.

" My stomach, it is not happy on the sea."

"Nonsense, man, it's a beautiful day. Calm as a mill pond. You can't let us down, you know."

Hercule Poirot hardly looked like responding to this British adjuration. But at that moment, Mrs. Castle poked her ladylike face and elaborate coiffure round the door.

"Ay'm sure ay hope ay am not intruding," she said. "But Mr. Lane, the clergyman, you know, has just returned. Ay thought you might like to know."

"Ah yes, thanks, Mrs. Castle. We'll see him right away."

Mrs. Castle came a little farther into the room. She said: "Ay don't know if it is worth mentioning, but ay *have* heard that the smallest incident should not be ignored——"

"Yes, yes?" said Weston impatiently.

"It is only that there was a lady and gentleman here about one o'clock. Came over from the mainland. For luncheon. They were informed that there had been an accident and that under the circumstances no luncheons could be served."

"Any idea who they were?"

"Ay couldn't say at all. Naturally no name was given. They expressed disappointment and a certain amount of curiosity as to the nature of the accident. Ay couldn't tell them anything, of course Ay should say, myself, they were summer visitors of the better class."

Weston said brusquely:

"Ah well, thank you for telling us. Probably not important but quite right—er—to remember everything."

"Naturally," said Mrs. Castle, "ay wish to do my Duty!"

"Quite, quite. Ask Mr. Lane to come here."

5

Stephen Lane strode into the room with his usual vigour.
Weston said:

"I'm the Chief Constable of the County, Mr. Lane. I suppose you've been told what has occurred here?"

"Yes—oh yes—I heard as soon as I got here Terrible. . . . Terrible. . . ." His thin frame quivered. He said in a low voice: "All along—ever since I arrived here—I have been conscious—very conscious—of the forces of evil close at hand."

His eyes, burning eager eyes, went to Hercule Poirot.
He said:

"You remember, M. Poirot? Our conversation some days
ago? About the reality of evil?"

Weston was studying the tall, gaunt figure in some per-
plexity. He found it difficult to make this man out. Lane's
eyes came back to him. The clergyman said with a slight
smile:

"I dare say that seems fantastic to you, sir. We have left off
believing in evil in these days. We have abolished Hell fire!
We no longer believe in the Devil! But Satan and Satan's
emissaries were never more powerful than they are to-day!"

Weston said:

"Er—er—yes, perhaps. That, Mr. Lane, is your province.
Mine is more prosaic—to clear up a case of murder."

Stephen Lane said:

"An awful word. Murder! One of the earliest sins known
on earth—the ruthless shedding of an innocent brother's
blood . . ." He paused, his eyes half closed. Then, in a
more ordinary voice he said:

"In what way can I help you?"

"First of all, Mr. Lane, will you tell me your own movements to-day?"

"Willingly. I started off early on one of my usual tramps.
I am fond of walking. I have roamed over a good deal of the
countryside round here. To-day I went to St. Petrock-in-the-
Combe. That is about seven miles from here—a very pleasant
walk along winding lanes, up and down the Devon hills and
valleys. I took some lunch with me and ate it in a spinney.
I visited the church—it has some fragments—only fragments
alas, of early glass—also a very interesting painted screen."

"Thank you, Mr. Lane. Did you meet any one on your
walk?"

"Not to speak to. A cart passed me once and a couple of
boys on bicycles and some cows. However," he smiled,
"if you want proof of my statement, I wrote my name in the
book at the church. You will find it there."

"You did not see any one at the church itself—the Vicar,
or the verger?"

Stephen Lane shook his head. He said:

"No, there was no one about and I was the only visitor.

St. Petrock is a very remote spot. The village itself lies on the far side of it about half a mile farther on."

Colonel Weston said pleasantly:

"You mustn't think we're—er—doubting what you say. Just a matter of checking-up on everybody. Just routine, you know, routine. Have to stick to routine in cases of this kind."

Stephen Lane said gently:

"Oh yes, I quite understand."

Weston went on:

"Now the next point. Is there anything you know that would assist us at all? Anything about the dead woman? Anything that could give us a pointer as to who murdered her? Anything you heard or saw?"

Stephen Lane said:

"I heard nothing. All I can tell you is this: that I knew instinctively as soon as I saw her that Arlena Marshall was a focus of evil. She *was* Evil! Evil personified! Woman can be man's help and inspiration in life—she can also be man's downfall. She can drag a man down to the level of the beast. The dead woman was just such a woman. She appealed to everything base in a man's nature. She was a woman such as Jezebel and Aholibah. Now—she has been struck down in the middle of her wickedness!"

Hercule Poirot stirred. He said:

"Not struck down—*strangled!* Strangled, Mr. Lane, by a pair of human hands."

The clergyman's own hands trembled. The fingers writhed and twitched. He said, and his voice came low and choked:

"That's horrible—horrible—— Must you put it like that?"

Hercule Poirot said:

"It is the simple truth. Have you any idea, Mr. Lane, whose hands those were?"

The other shook his head. He said: "I know nothing—nothing . . ."

Weston got up. He said, after a glance at Colgate to which the latter replied by an almost imperceptible nod, "Well, we must get on to the Cove."

Lane said:

"Is that where—it happened?"

Weston nodded.

Lane said:

" Can—can I come with you?"

About to return a curt negative, Weston was forestalled by Poirot.

" But certainly," said Poirot. " Accompany me there in a boat, Mr. Lane. We start immediately."

Chapter Nine

1

FOR the second time that morning Patrick Redfern was rowing a boat into Pixy's Cove. The other occupants of the boat were Hercule Poirot, very pale with a hand to his stomach, and Stephen Lane. Colonel Weston had taken the land route. Having been delayed on the way he arrived on the beach at the same time as the boat grounded. A police constable and a plain-clothes sergeant were on the beach already. Weston was questioning the latter as the three from the boat walked up and joined him.

Sergeant Phillips said:

" I think I've been over every inch of the beach, sir."

" Good, what did you find?"

" It's all together here, sir, if you'd like to come and see."

A small collection of objects was laid out neatly on a rock. There was a pair of scissors, an empty gold flake packet, five patent bottle tops, a number of used matches, three pieces of string, one or two fragments of newspaper, a fragment of a smashed pipe, four buttons, the drumstick bone of a chicken and an empty bottle of sun-bathing oil.

Weston looked down appraisingly on the objects.

" H'm." he said. " Rather moderate for a beach nowadays! Most people seem to confuse a beach with a public rubbish dump! Empty bottle's been here some time by the way the label's blurred—so have most of the other things, I should say. The scissors are new, though. Bright and shining. *They* weren't out in yesterday's rain! Where were they?"

" Close by the bottom of the ladder, sir. Also this bit of pipe."

" H'm, probably dropped by someone going up or down. Nothing to say who they belong to?"

" No, sir. Quite an ordinary pair of nail scissors. Pipe's a good quality brier—expensive."

Poirot murmured thoughtfully:

" Captain Marshall told us, I think, that he had mislaid his pipe."

Weston said:

" Marshall's out of the picture. Anyway, he's not the only person who smokes a pipe."

Hercule Poirot was watching Stephen Lane as the latter's hand went to his pocket and away again. He said pleasantly:

" You also smoke a pipe, do you not, Mr. Lane?"

The clergyman started. He looked at Poirot.

He said:

" Yes. Oh yes. My pipe is an old friend and companion." Putting his hand into his pocket again he drew out a pipe, filled it with tobacco and lighted it.

Hercule Poirot moved away to where Redfern was standing, his eyes blank.

He said in a low voice:

" I'm glad—they've taken *her* away . . ."

Stephen Lane asked:

" Where was she found?"

The Sergeant said cheerfully:

" Just about where you're standing, sir."

Lane moved swiftly aside. He stared at the spot he had just vacated.

The Sergeant went on:

" Place where the float was drawn up agrees with putting the time she arrived here at 10.45. That's going by the tide. It's turned now."

" Photography all done?" asked Weston.

" Yes, sir."

Weston turned to Redfern.

" Now then, man, where's the entrance to this cave of yours?"

Patrick Redfern was still staring down at the beach where Lane had been standing. It was as though he was seeing that sprawling body that was no longer there.

Weston's words recalled him to himself.

He said: " It's over here."

He led the way to where a great mass of tumbled-down rocks were massed picturesquely against the cliff side. He went straight to where two big rocks, side by side, showed a straight narrow cleft between them. He said:

"The entrance is here."

Weston said:

"Here? Doesn't look as though a man could squeeze through."

"It's deceptive, you'll find, sir. It can just be done."

Weston inserted himself gingerly into the cleft. It was not as narrow as it looked. Inside, the space widened and proved to be a fairly roomy recess with room to stand upright and to move about.

Hercule Poirot and Stephen Lane joined the Chief Constable. The other stayed outside. Light filtered in through the opening, but Weston had also got a powerful torch which he played freely over the interior.

He observed:

"Handy place. You'd never suspect it from the outside."

He played the torch carefully over the floor.

Hercule Poirot was delicately sniffing the air.

Noticing this, Weston said:

"Air quite fresh, not fishy or seaweedy, but of course this place is well above high water mark."

But to Poirot's sensitive nose, the air was more than fresh. It was delicately scented. He knew two people who used that elusive perfume . . .

Weston's torch came to rest. He said:

"Don't see anything out of the way in here."

Poirot's eyes rose to a ledge a little way above his head. He murmured:

"One might perhaps see that there is nothing up there?"

Weston said: "If there's anything up there it would have to be deliberately put there. Still, we'd better have a look."

Poirot said to Lane:

"You are, I think, the tallest of us, Monsieur. Could we venture to ask you to make sure there is nothing resting on that ledge?"

Lane stretched up, but he could not quite reach to the back of the shelf. Then, seeing a crevice in the rock, he inserted a toe in it and pulled himself up by one hand.

He said:

"Hullo, there's a box up here."

In a minute or two they were out in the sunshine examining the clergyman's find.

Weston said:

"Careful, don't handle it more than you can help. May be finger-prints."

It was a dark-green tin box and bore the word Sandwiches on it.

Sergeant Phillips said:

"Left from some picnic or other, I suppose."

He opened the lid with his handkerchief.

Inside were small tin containers marked salt, pepper, mustard and two larger square tins evidently for sandwiches. Sergeant Phillips lifted the lid of the salt container. It was full to the brim. He raised the next one, commenting:

"H'm, got salt in the pepper one too."

The mustard compartment also contained salt.

His face suddenly alert, the police sergeant opened one of the bigger square tins. That, too, contained the same white crystalline powder.

Very gingerly, Sergeant Phillips dipped a finger in and applied it to his tongue.

His face changed. He said—and his voice was excited:

"This isn't *salt*, sir. Not by a long way! Bitter taste! Seems to me it's some kind of *drug*."

2

"The third angle," said Colonel Weston with a groan.

They were back at the hotel again.

The Chief Constable went on:

"If by any chance there's a dope gang mixed up in this, it opens up several possibilities. First of all, the dead woman may have been in with the gang herself. Think that's likely?"

Hercule Poirot said cautiously:

"It is possible."

"She may have been a drug addict?"

Poirot shook his head.

He said:

"I should doubt that. She had steady nerves, radiant health, there were no marks of hypodermic injections (not that

E

that proves anything. Some people sniff the stuff). No, I do not think she took drugs."

"In that case," said Weston, "she may have run into the business accidentally, and she was deliberately silenced by the people running the show. We'll know presently just what the stuff is. I've sent it to Neasdon. If we're on to some dope ring, they're not the people to stick at trifles——"

He broke off as the door opened and Mr. Horace Blatt came briskly into the room.

Mr. Blatt was looking hot. He was wiping the perspiration from his forehead. His big hearty voice billowed out and filled the small room.

"Just this minute got back and heard the news! You the Chief Constable? They told me you were in here. My name's Blatt—Horace Blatt. Any way I can help you? Don't suppose so. I've been out in my boat since early this morning. Missed the whole blinking show. The one day that something *does* happen in this out-of-the-way spot, I'm not there. Just like life, that, isn't it? Hullo, Poirot, didn't see you at first. So you're in on this? Oh well, I suppose you would be. Sherlock Holmes *v.* the local police, is that it? Ha, ha! Lestrade—all that stuff. I'll enjoy seeing you do a bit of fancy sleuthing."

Mr. Blatt came to anchor in a chair, pulled out a cigarette case and offered it to Colonel Weston, who shook his head.

He said, with a slight smile:

"I'm an inveterate pipe smoker."

"Same here. I smoke cigarettes as well—but nothing beats a pipe."

Colonel Weston said with sudden geniality:

"Then light up, man."

Blatt shook his head.

"Not got my pipe on me at the moment. But put me wise about all this. All I've heard so far is that Mrs. Marshall was found murdered on one of the beaches here."

"On Pixy Cove," said Colonel Weston, watching him.

But Mr. Blatt merely asked excitedly:

"And she was strangled?"

"Yes, Mr. Blatt."

"Nasty—very nasty. Mind you, she asked for it! Hot stuff—*trés moutarde*—eh, M. Poirot? Any idea who did it, or mustn't I ask that?"

With a faint smile Colonel Weston said:

"Well, you know, it's we who are supposed to ask the questions."

Mr. Blatt waved his cigarette.

"Sorry—sorry—my mistake. Go ahead."

"You went out sailing this morning. At what time?"

"Left here at a quarter to ten."

"Was any one with you?"

"Not a soul. All on my little lonesome."

"And where did you go?"

"Along the coast in the direction of Plymouth. Took lunch with me. Not much wind so I didn't actually get very far."

After another question or two, Weston asked:

"Now about the Marshalls? Do you know anything that might help us?"

"Well, I've given you my opinion. *Crime passionnel!* All I can tell you is, it wasn't *me!* The fair Arlena had no use for me. Nothing doing in that quarter. She had her own blue-eyed boy! And if you ask me, Marshall was getting wise to it."

"Have you any evidence for that?"

"Saw him give young Redfern a dirty look once or twice. Dark horse, Marshall. Looks very meek and mild and as though he were half asleep all the time—but that's not his reputation in the City. I've heard a thing or two about him. Nearly had up for assault once. Mind you, the fellow in question had put up a pretty dirty deal. Marshall had trusted him and the fellow had let him down cold. Particularly dirty business, I believe. Marshall went for him and half killed him Fellow didn't prosecute—too afraid of what might come out. I give you that for what it's worth."

"So you think it possible," said Poirot, "that Captain Marshall strangled his wife?"

"Not at all. Never said anything of the sort. Just letting you know that he's the sort of fellow who could go berserk on occasions."

Poirot said:

"Mr. Blatt, there is reason to believe that Mrs. Marshall went this morning to Pixy Cove to meet someone. Have you any idea who that someone might be?"

Mr. Blatt winked.

"It's not a guess. It's a certainty. Redfern!"

"It was not Mr. Redfern."

Mr. Blatt seemed taken aback. He said hesitatingly.

"Then I don't know . . . No, I can't imagine . . ."

He went on, regaining a little of his aplomb:

"As I said before, it wasn't *me*! No such luck! Let me see, couldn't have been Gardener—his wife keeps far too sharp an eye on him! That old ass Barry? Rot! And it would hardly be the parson. Although, mind you, I've seen his Reverence watching her a good bit. All holy disapproval, but perhaps an eye for the contours all the same! Eh? Lot of hypocrites, most parsons. Did you read that case last month? Parson and the churchwarden's daughter! Bit of an eye-opener."

Mr. Blatt chuckled.

Colonel Weston said coldly:

"There is nothing you can think of that might help us?"

The other shook his head.

"No. Can't think of a thing." He added: "This will make a bit of a stir, I imagine. The Press will be on to it like hot cakes. There won't be quite so much of this high-toned exclusiveness about the Jolly Roger in future. Jolly Roger indeed. Precious little jollity about it."

Hercule Poirot murmured:

"You have not enjoyed your stay here?"

Mr. Blatt's red face got slightly redder. He said:

"Well, no, I haven't. The sailing's all right and the scenery and the service and the food—but there's no *matiness* in the place, you know what I mean! What I say is, my money's as good as another man's. We're all here to enjoy ourselves. Then why not get together and *do* it? All these cliques and people sitting by themselves and giving you frosty good-mornings—and good-evenings—and yes, very pleasant weather. No joy de viver. Lot of stuck-up dummies!"

Mr. Blatt paused—by now very red indeed.

He wiped his forehead once more and said apologetically:

"Don't pay any attention to me. I get all worked up."

3

Hercule Poirot murmured:

" And what do we think of Mr. Blatt?"

Colonel Weston grinned and said:

" What do *you* think of him? You've seen more of him than I have."

Poirot said softly:

" There are many of your English idioms that describe him. The rough diamond! The self-made man! The social climber! He is, as you choose to look at it, pathetic, ludicrous, blatant! It is a matter of opinion. But I think, too, that he is something else."

" And what is that?"

Hercule Poirot, his eyes raised to the ceiling, murmured:

" I think that he is—*nervous!*"

4

Inspector Colgate said:

" I've got those times worked out. From the hotel to the ladder down to Pixy Cove three minutes. That's walking till you are out of sight of the hotel and then running like hell."

Weston raised his eyebrows. He said:

" That's quicker than I thought."

" Down ladder to beach one minute and three-quarters. Up same two minutes. That's P.C. Flint. He's a bit of an athlete. Walking and taking the ladder in the normal way, the whole business takes close on a quarter of an hour."

Weston nodded. He said:

" There's another thing we must go into, the pipe question."

Colgate said:

" Blatt smokes a pipe, so does Marshall, so does the parson. Redfern smokes cigarettes, the American prefers a cigar. Major Barry doesn't smoke at all. There's one pipe in Marshall's room, two in Blatt's, and one in the parson's. Chambermaid says Marshall has two pipes. The other chambermaid isn't a very bright girl. Doesn't know how many pipes the other two have. Says vaguely she's noticed two or three about in their rooms."

Weston nodded.

" Anything else?"

" I've checked up on the staff. They all seem quite O.K. Henry, in the bar, checks Marshall's statement about seeing him at ten to eleven. William, the beach attendant, was down repairing the ladder on the rocks by the hotel most of the morning. He seems all right. George marked the tennis court and then bedded out some plants round by the dining-room. Neither of them would have seen any one who came across the causeway to the island."

" When was the causeway uncovered?"

" Round about 9.30, sir."

Weston pulled at his moustache.

" It's possible somebody did come that way. We've got a new angle, Colgate."

He told of the discovery of the sandwich box in the cave.

5

There was a tap on the door.

" Come in," said Weston.

It was Captain Marshall.

He said:

" Can you tell me what arrangements I can make about the funeral?"

" I think we shall manage the inquest for the day after to-morrow, Captain Marshall."

" Thank you."

Inspector Colgate said:

" Excuse me, sir, allow me to return you these."

He handed over the three letters.

Kenneth Marshall smiled rather sardonically.

He said:

" Has the police department been testing the speed of my typing? I hope my character is cleared."

Colonel Weston said pleasantly.

" Yes, Captain Marshall, I think we can give you a clean bill of health. Those sheets take fully an hour to type. Moreover you were heard typing them by the chambermaid up till five minutes to eleven and you were seen by another witness at twenty minutes past."

Captain Marshall murmured:

"Really? That all seems very satisfactory!"

"Yes. Miss Darnley came to your room at twenty minutes past eleven. You were so busy typing that you did not observe her entry."

Kenneth Marshall's face took on an impassive expression. He said:

"Does Miss Darnley say that?" He paused. "As a matter of fact she is wrong. I *did* see her, though she may not be aware of the fact. I saw her in the mirror."

Poirot murmured:

"But you did not interrupt your typing?"

Marshall said shortly:

"No. I wanted to get finished."

He paused a minute, then, in an abrupt voice, he said:

"Nothing more I can do for you?"

"No, thank you, Captain Marshall."

Kenneth Marshall nodded and went out.

Weston said with a sigh:

"There goes our most hopeful suspect—cleared! Hullo, here's Neasdon."

The doctor came in with a trace of excitement in his manner. He said:

"That's a nice little death lot you sent me along."

"What is it?"

"What is it? Diamorphine Hydrochloride. Stuff that's usually called Heroin."

Inspector Colgate whistled. He said:

"Now we're getting places, all right! Depend upon it, this dope stunt is at the bottom of the whole business."

Chapter Ten

THE little crowd of people flocked out of the Red Bull. The brief inquest was over—adjourned for a fortnight.

Rosamund Darnley joined Captain Marshall. She said in a low voice:

"That wasn't so bad. was it, Ken?"

He did not answer at once. Perhaps he was conscious of the staring eyes of the villagers, the fingers that nearly pointed to him and only just did not quite do so!

"*That's 'im, my dear.*" "*See, that's 'er 'usband.*" "*That be the 'usband.*" "*Look, there 'e goes . . .*"

The murmurs were not loud enough to reach his ears, but he was none the less sensitive to them. This was the modern-day pillory. The Press he had already encountered—self-confident, persuasive young men, adepts at battering down his wall of silence of " Nothing to say " that he had endeavoured to erect. Even the curt monosyllables that he had uttered, thinking that they at least could not lead to misapprehension, had reappeared in his morning's papers in a totally different guise. " Asked whether he agreed that the mystery of his wife's death could only be explained on the assumption that a homicidal murderer had found his way on to the island, Captain Marshall declared that——" and so on and so forth.

Cameras had clicked ceaselessly. Now, at this minute, the well-known sound caught his ear. He half turned—a smiling young man was nodding cheerfully, his purpose accomplished.

Rosamund murmured:

"*Captain Marshall and a friend leaving the Red Bull after the inquest.*"

Marshall winced.

Rosamund said:

"It's no use, Ken! You've got to face it! I don't mean just the fact of Arlena's death—I mean all the attendant beastliness. The staring eyes and gossiping tongues, the fatuous interviews in the papers—and the best way to meet it is

to find it funny! Come out with all the old inane cliches
and curl a sardonic lip at them."

He said:

" Is that your way?"

" Yes." She paused. " It isn't yours, I know. Protective
colouring is your line. Remain rigidly non-active and fade
into the background! But you can't do that here—you've no
background to fade into. You stand out clear for all to see
—like a striped tiger against a white backcloth. *The husband
of the murdered woman!*"

" For God's sake, Rosamund——"

She said gently:

" My dear, I'm trying to be good for you!"

They walked for a few steps in silence. Then Marshall said
in a different voice:

" I know you are. I'm not really ungrateful, Rosamund."

They had progressed beyond the limits of the village. Eyes
followed them but there was no one very near. Rosamund
Darnley's voice dropped as she repeated a variant of her first
remark.

" It didn't really go so badly, did it?"

He was silent for a moment, then he said:

" I don't know."

" What do the police think?"

" They're non-committal."

After a minute Rosamund said:

" That little man—Poirot—is he really taking an active
interest?"

Kenneth Marshall said:

" Seemed to be sitting in the Chief Constable's pocket all
right the other day."

" I know—but is he *doing* anything?"

" How the hell should I know, Rosamund?"

She said thoughtfully:

" He's pretty old. Probably more or less ga ga."

" Perhaps."

They came to the causeway. Opposite them, serene in the
sun, lay the island.

Rosamund said suddenly:

" Sometimes—things seem unreal. I can't believe, this
minute, that it ever happened . . ."

Marshall said slowly:

"I think I know what you mean. Nature is so regardless! One ant the less—that's all it is in Nature!"

Rosamund said:

"Yes—and that's the proper way to look at it really."

He gave her one very quick glance. Then he said in a low voice:

"Don't worry, my dear. It's all right. *It's all right.*"

2

Linda came down to the causeway to meet them. She moved with the spasmodic jerkiness of a nervous colt. Her young face was marred by deep black shadows under her eyes. Her lips were dry and rough.

She said breathlessly:

"What happened—what—what did they say?"

Her father said abruptly:

"Inquest adjourned for a fortnight."

"That means they—they haven't decided?"

"Yes More evidence is needed."

"But—but what do they think?"

Marshall smiled a little in spite of himself.

"Oh, my dear child—who knows? And whom do you mean by they? The coroner, the jury, the police, the newspaper reporters, the fishing folk of Leathercombe Bay?"

Linda said slowly·

"I suppose I mean—the police."

Marshall said dryly:

"Whatever the police think, they're not giving it away at present."

His lips closed tightly after the sentence. He went into the hotel.

As Rosamund Darnley was about to follow suit, Linda said:

"Rosamund!"

Rosamund turned. The mute appeal in the girl's unhappy face touched her. She linked her arm through Linda's and together they walked away from the hotel, taking the path that led to the extreme end of the island.

Rosamund said gently:

"Try not to mind so much, Linda. I know it's all very

terrible and a shock and all that, but it's no use brooding over these things. And it can be only the—horror of it, that is worrying you. You weren't in the least *fond* of Arlena, you know."

She felt the tremor that ran through the girl's body as Linda answered:

" No, I wasn't fond of her . . ."

Rosamund went on:

" Sorrow for a person is different—one can't put *that* behind one. But one *can* get over shock and horror by just not letting your mind *dwell* on it all the time."

Linda said sharply:

" You don't understand."

" I think I do, my dear."

Linda shook her head.

" No, you don't. You don't understand in the least—and Christine doesn't understand either! Both of you have been nice to me, but you can't understand what I'm feeling. You just think it's morbid—that I'm dwelling on it all when I needn't."

She paused.

" But it isn't that at all. If you knew what I know——"

Rosamund stopped dead. Her body did not tremble—on the contrary it stiffened. She stood for a minute or two, then she disengaged her arm from Linda's.

She said:

" What is it that you know, Linda?"

The girl gazed at her. Then she shook her head.

She muttered:

" Nothing."

Rosamund caught her by the arm. The grip hurt and Linda winced slightly.

Rosamund said:

" Be careful, Linda. Be damned careful."

Linda had gone dead white.

She said:

" I *am* very careful—all the time."

Rosamund said urgently:

" Listen, Linda, what I said a minute or two ago applies just the same—only a hundred times more so. *Put the whole business out of your mind.* Never think about it. Forget—forget . . . You can if you try! Arlena is dead and nothing

can bring her back to life . . . Forget everything and live in
the future. And above all, *hold your tongue.*"

Linda shrank a little. She said:

"You—you seem to know all about it?"

Rosamund said energetically:

"I don't know *anything!* In my opinion a wandering maniac
got on to the island and killed Arlena. That's much the most
probable solution. I'm fairly sure that the police will have to
accept that in the end. That's what *must* have happened!
That's what *did* happen!"

Linda said:

"If Father——"

Rosamund interrupted her.

"Don't talk about it."

Linda said:

"I've got to say one thing. My mother——"

"Well, what about her?"

"She—she was tried for murder, wasn't she?"

"Yes."

Linda said slowly:

"And then Father married her. That looks, doesn't it, as
though Father didn't really think murder was very wrong—not
always, that is."

Rosamund said sharply:

"Don't say things like that—even to me! The police
haven't got anything against your father. He's got an alibi—
an alibi that they can't break. He's perfectly safe."

Linda whispered:

"Did they think at first that Father——?"

Rosamund cried:

"I don't know what they thought! But they know now *that
he couldn't have done it.* Do you understand? *He couldn't
have done it.*"

She spoke with authority, her eyes commanded Linda's
acquiescence. The girl uttered a long fluttering sigh.

Rosamund said:

"You'll be able to leave here soon. You'll forget everything—everything!"

Linda said with sudden unexpected violence.

"*I shall never forget.*"

She turned abruptly and ran back to the hotel. Rosamund
stared after her.

3

"There is something I want to know, Madame?"

Christine Redfern glanced up at Poirot in a slightly abstracted manner. She said:

"Yes?"

Hercule Poirot took very little notice of her abstraction. He had noted the way her eyes followed her husband's figure where he was pacing up and down on the terrace outside the bar, but for the moment he had no interest in purely conjugal problems. He wanted information.

He said:

"Yes, Madame. It was a phrase—a chance phrase of yours the other day which roused my attention."

Christine, her eyes still on Patrick, said:

"Yes? What did I say?"

"It was in answer to a question from the Chief Constable. You described how you went into Miss Linda Marshall's room on the morning of the crime and how you found her absent from it and how she returned there, and it was then that the Chief Constable asked you where she had been."

Christine said rather impatiently:

"And I said she had been bathing? Is that it?"

"Ah, but you did not say quite that. You did not say 'she had been bathing.' Your words were, 'she said she had been bathing.'"

Christine said:

"It's the same thing, surely."

"No, it is not the same! The form of your answer suggests a certain attitude of mind on your part. Linda Marshall came into the room—she was wearing a bathing-wrap and yet—for some reason—you did not at once assume she had been bathing. That is shown by your words, 'she *said* she had been bathing.' What was there about her appearance—was it her manner, or something that she was wearing or something she said—that led you to feel surprised when she said she had been bathing?"

Christine's attention left Patrick and focused itself entirely on Poirot. She was interested. She said:

"That's clever of you. It's quite true, now I remember. . . .

I *was*, just faintly, surprised when Linda said she had been bathing."

" But why, Madame, why?"

" Yes, why? That's just what I'm trying to remember. Oh yes, I think it was the parcel in her hand."

" She had a parcel?"

" Yes "

" You do not know what was in it?"

" Oh yes, I do. The string broke. It was loosely done up in the way they do in the village. It was *candles*—they were scattered on the floor. I helped her to pick them up."

" Ah," said Poirot. " Candles."

Christine stared at him. She said:

" You seem excited, M. Poirot."

Poirot asked:

" Did Linda say why she had bought candles?"

Christine reflected.

" No, I don't think she did. I suppose it was to read by at night—perhaps the electric light wasn't good."

" On the contrary, Madame, there was a bedside electric lamp in perfect order."

Christine said:

" Then I don't know what she wanted them for."

Poirot said:

" What was her manner—when the string broke and the candles fell out of the parcel?"

Christine said slowly:

" She was—upset—embarrassed."

Poirot nodded his head. Then he asked:

" Did you notice a calendar in her room?"

" A calendar? What kind of a calendar?"

Poirot said:

" Possibly a green calendar—with tear-off leaves."

Christine screwed up her eyes in an effort of memory.

" A green calendar—rather a bright green. Yes, I have seen a calendar like that—but I can't remember where. It may have been in Linda's room, but I can't be sure."

" But you have definitely seen such a thing."

" Yes."

Again Poirot nodded.

Christine said rather sharply:

"What are you hinting at, M. Poirot? What is the meaning of all this?"

For answer Poirot produced a small volume bound in faded brown calf. He said:

"Have you ever seen this before?"

"Why—I think—I'm not sure—yes, Linda was looking into it in the village lending library the other day. But she shut it up and thrust it back quickly when I came up to her. It made me wonder what it was."

Silently Poirot displayed the title.

A History of Witchcraft, Sorcery and of the Compounding of Untraceable Poisons.

Christine said:

"I don't understand. What does all this mean?"

Poirot said gravely.

"It may mean, Madame, a good deal."

She looked at him inquiringly, but he did not go on. Instead he asked:

"One more question, Madame, did you take a bath that morning before you went out to play tennis?"

Christine stared again.

"A bath? No. I would have had no time and, anyway, I didn't want a bath—not before tennis. I might have had one after."

"Did you use your bathroom at all when you came in?"

"I sponged my face and hands, that's all."

"You did not turn on the bath at all?"

"No, I'm sure I didn't."

Poirot nodded. He said:

"It is of no importance."

4

Hercule Poirot stood by the table where Mrs. Gardener was wrestling with a jig-saw. She looked up and jumped.

"Why, M. Poirot, how very quietly you came up beside me! I never heard you. Have you just come back from the inquest? You know, the very thought of that inquest makes me so nervous, I don't know what to do. That's why I'm doing this puzzle. I just felt I couldn't sit outside on the

beach as usual. As Mr. Gardener knows, when my nerves
are all upset, there's nothing like one of these puzzles for
calming me. There now, where *does* this white piece fit in? It
must be part of the fur rug, but I don't seem to see . . ."

Gently Poirot's hand took the piece from her. He said:

" It fits, Madame, *here*. It is part of the cat."

" It can't be. It's a black cat."

" A black cat, yes, but you see the tip of the black cat's tail
happens to be white."

" Why, so it does! How clever of you! But I do think the
people who make puzzles are kind of mean. They just go
out of their way to deceive you."

She fitted in another piece and then resumed.

" You know, M. Poirot, I've been watching you this last day
or two. I just wanted to watch you detecting if you know
what I mean—not that it doesn't sound rather heartless put
like that, as though it were all a game—and a poor creature
killed. Oh dear, every time *I* think of it I get the shivers! I
told Mr. Gardener this morning I'd just *got* to get away
from here, and now the inquest's over he thinks we'll be able
to leave to-morrow, and that's a blessing, I'm sure. But about
detecting, I would so like to know your methods—you know,
I'd feel privileged if you'd just *explain* it to me."

Hercule Poirot said:

" It is a little like your puzzle, Madame. One assembles the
pieces. It is like a mosaic—many colours and patterns—and
every strange-shaped little piece must be fitted into its own
place."

" Now isn't that interesting? Why, I'm sure you explain it
just too beautifully."

Poirot went on:

" And sometimes it is like that piece of your puzzle just
now. One arranges very methodically the pieces of the
puzzle—one sorts the colours—and then perhaps a piece
of one colour that should fit in with—say, the fur rug, fits in
instead in a black cat's tail."

" Why, if that doesn't sound too fascinating! And are there
a great many pieces, M. Poirot?"

" Yes, Madame. Almost every one here in this hotel has
given me a piece for my puzzle. You amongst them."

" Me?" Mrs. Gardener's tone was shrill.

"Yes, a remark of yours, Madame, was exceedingly helpful. I might say it was illuminating."

"Well, if that isn't too lovely! Can't you tell me some more, M. Poirot?"

"Ah! Madame, I reserve the explanations for the last chapter."

Mrs. Gardener murmured:

"If that isn't just too bad!"

5

Hercule Poirot tapped gently on the door of Captain Marshall's room. Inside there was the sound of a typewriter.

A curt "Come in" came from the room and Poirot entered.

Captain Marshall's back was turned to him. He was sitting typing at the table between the windows. He did not turn his head but his eyes met Poirot's in the mirror that hung on the wall directly in front of him. He said irritably:

"Well, M. Poirot, what is it?"

Poirot said quickly:

"A thousand apologies for intruding. You are busy?"

Marshall said shortly: "I am rather."

Poirot said:

"It is one little question that I would like to ask you."

Marshall said:

"My God, I'm sick of answering questions. I've answered the police questions. I don't feel called upon to answer yours."

Poirot said:

"Mine is a very simple one. Only this. On the morning of your wife's death, did you have a bath after you finished typing and before you went out to play tennis?"

"A bath? No, of course I didn't! I'd had a bathe only an hour earlier!"

Hercule Poirot said:

"Thank you. That is all."

"But look here. Oh——" the other paused irresolutely.

Poirot withdrew, gently closing the door.

Kenneth Marshall said:

"The fellow's crazy!"

6

Just outside the bar Poirot encountered Mr. Gardener. He was carrying two cocktails and was clearly on his way to where Mrs. Gardener was ensconced with her jig-saw.

He smiled at Poirot in genial fashion.

" Care to join us, M. Poirot?"

Poirot shook his head. He said:

" What did you think of the inquest, Mr. Gardener?"

Mr. Gardener lowered his voice. He said:

" Seemed kind of indeterminate to me. Your police, I gather, have got something up their sleeves."

" It is possible," said Hercule Poirot.

Mr. Gardener lowered his voice still further.

" I shall be glad to get Mrs. Gardener away. She's a very, very sensitive woman, and this affair has got on her nerves. She's very highly strung."

Hercule Poirot said:

" Will you permit me, Mr. Gardener, to ask you one question?"

" Why, certainly, M. Poirot. Delighted to assist in any way I can."

Hercule Poirot said:

" You are a man of the world—a man, I think, of considerable acumen. What, frankly, was your opinion of the late Mrs. Marshall?"

Mr. Gardener's eyebrows rose in surprise. He glanced cautiously round and lowered his voice.

" Well, M. Poirot, I've heard a few things that have been kind of going around, if you get me, especially among the women " Poirot nodded. " But if you ask me I'll tell you my candid opinion and that is that that woman was pretty much of a darned fool!"

Hercule Poirot said thoughtfully:

" Now that is very interesting."

7

Rosamund Darnley said: " So it's my turn, is it?"
" Pardon?"
She laughed.
" The other day the Chief Constable held his inquisition.
You sat by. To-day, I think, you are conducting your own
unofficial inquiry. I've been watching you. First Mrs. Redfern, then I caught a glimpse of you through the lounge
window where Mrs. Gardener is doing her hateful jig-saw
puzzle. Now it's my turn."

Hercule Poirot sat down beside her. They were on
Sunny Ledge. Below them the sea showed a deep-glowing
green. Farther out it was a pale dazzling blue.

Poirot said:

" You are very intelligent, Mademoiselle. I have thought so
ever since I arrived here. It would be a pleasure to discuss
this business with you."

Rosamund Darnley said softly:

" You want to know what I think about the whole thing?"
" It would be most interesting."

Rosamund said:

" I think it's really very simple. The clue is in the woman's
past."
" The past? Not the present?"
" Oh! not necessarily the very remote past. I look at it
like this. Arlena Marshall was attractive, fatally attractive,
to men It's possible, I think, that she also tired of them
rather quickly. Amongst her—followers, shall we say—
was one who resented that. Oh, don't misunderstand me, it
won't be someone who sticks out a mile. Probably some
tepid little man, vain and sensitive—the kind of man who
broods. I think he followed her down here, waited his
opportunity and killed her."

" You mean that he was an outsider, that he came from the
mainland?"

" Yes. He probably hid in that cave until he got his
chance."

Poirot shook his head. He said:

" Would she go there to meet such a man as you
describe? No, she would laugh and not go."

Rosamund said:

" She mayn't have known she was going to meet him. He may have sent her a message in some other person's name."

Poirot murmured:

" That is possible."

Then he said:

" But you forget one thing, Mademoiselle. A man bent on murder could not risk coming in broad daylight across the causeway and past the hotel. Someone might have seen him."

" They might have—but I don't think that it's certain. I think it's quite possible that he could have come without any one noticing him at all."

" It would be *possible*, yes, that I grant you. But the point is that he could not *count* on that possibility."

Rosamund said:

" Aren't you forgetting something? The weather."

" The weather?"

" Yes. The day of the murder was a glorious day, but the day before, remember, there was rain and thick mist. Any one could come on to the island then without being seen. He had only to go down to the beach and spend the night in the cave. That mist, M. Poirot, is important."

Poirot looked at her thoughtfully for a minute or two. He said:

" You know, there is a good deal in what you have just said."

Rosamund flushed. She said:

" That's my theory, for what it is worth. Now tell me yours."

" Ah," said Hercule Poirot. He stared down at the sea.

" *Eh bien*, Mademoiselle. I am a very simple person. I always incline to the belief that the most likely person committed the crime. At the very beginning it seemed to me that one person was very clearly indicated."

Rosamund's voice hardened a little. She said:

" Go on."

Hercule Poirot went on.

" But you see, there is what you call a snag in the way! It seems that it was *impossible* for that person to have committed the crime "

He heard the quick expulsion of her breath. She said rather breathlessly:

" Well?"

Hercule Poirot shrugged his shoulders.

" Well, what do we do about it? That is my problem."
He paused and then went on " May I ask you a question?"

" Certainly."

She faced him, alert and vigilant. But the question that
came was an unexpected one.

" When you came in to change for tennis that morning,
did you have a bath?"

Rosamund stared at him.

" A bath? What do you mean?"

" That is what I mean. A bath! The receptacle of
porcelain, one turns the taps and fills it, one gets in, one
gets out and ghoosh—ghoosh—ghoosh, the water goes down
the waste-pipe!"

" M. Poirot, are you quite mad?"

" No, I ame extremely sane."

" Well, anyway, I *didn't* take a bath."

" Ha!" said Poirot. " So nobody took a bath. That is
extremely interesting."

" But why should any one take a bath?"

Hercule Poirot said: " Why, indeed?"

Rosamund said with some exasperation:

" I suppose this is the Sherlock Holmes touch!"

Hercule Poirot smiled.

Then he sniffed the air delicately.

" Will you permit me to be impertinent, Mademoiselle?"

" I'm sure you couldn't be impertinent, M. Poirot."

" That is very kind of you. Then may I venture to say that
the scent you use is delicious—it has a *nuance*—a delicate
elusive charm." He waved his hands, and then added in a
practical voice, " Gabrielle, No. 8, I think?"

" How clever you are. Yes, I always use it."

" So did the late Mrs. Marshall. It is chic, eh? And very
expensive?"

Rosamund shrugged her shoulders with a faint smile.

Poirot said:

" You sat here where we are now, Mademoiselle, on the
morning of the crime. You were seen here, or at least your
sunshade was seen by Miss Brewster and Mr. Redfern as
they passed on the sea. During the morning, Mademoiselle,

are you sure you did not happen to go down to Pixy's Cove and enter the cave there—the famous Pixy's Cave?"

Rosamund turned her head and stared at him.

She said in a quiet level voice.

"Are you asking me if I killed Arlena Marshall?"

"No, I am asking you if you went into the Pixy's Cave?"

"I don't even know where it is. Why should I go into it? For what reason?"

"On the day of the crime, Mademoiselle, somebody had been in that cave who used Gabrielle No. 8."

Rosamund said sharply.

"You've just said yourself, M. Poirot, that Arlena Marshall used Gabrielle No. 8. She was on the beach there that day. Presumably she went into the cave"

"Why should she go into the cave? It is dark there and narrow and very uncomfortable."

Rosamund said impatiently:

"Don't ask me for reasons. Since she was actually at the cove she was by far the most likely person. I've told you already I never left this place the whole morning."

"Except for the time when you went into the hotel to Captain Marshall's room." Poirot reminded her.

"Yes, of course. I'd forgotten that."

Poirot said:

"And you were wrong, Mademoiselle, when you thought that Captain Marshall did not see you."

Rosamund said incredulously:

"Kenneth did see me? Did—did he say so?"

Poirot nodded.

"He saw you, Mademoiselle, in the mirror that hangs over the table."

Rosamund caught her breath. She said:

"Oh! I see."

Poirot was no longer looking out to sea. He was looking at Rosamund Darnley's hands as they lay folded in her lap. They were well-shaped hands, beautifully moulded with very long fingers.

Rosamund, shooting a quick look at him, followed the direction of his eyes. She said sharply:

"What are you looking at my hands for? Do you think— do you think——?"

Poirot said:

" Do I think—what, Mademoiselle?"

Rosamund Darnley said:

" Nothing."

It was perhaps an hour later that Hercule Poirot came to the top of the path leading to Gull Cove. There was someone sitting on the beach. A slight figure in a red shirt and dark blue shorts.

Poirot descended the path, stepping carefully in his tight smart shoes.

Linda Marshall turned her head sharply. He thought that she shrank a little.

Her eyes, as he came and lowered himself gingerly to the shingle beside her, rested on him with the suspicion and alertness of a trapped animal. He realised, with a pang, how young and vulnerable she was.

She said:

" What is it? What do you want?"

Hercule Poirot did not answer for a minute or two. Then he said:

" The other day you told the Chief Constable that you were fond of your stepmother and that she was kind to you."

" Well?"

" That was not true, was it, Mademoiselle?"

" Yes, it was."

Poirot said:

" She may not have been actively unkind—that I will grant. But you were not fond of her—— Oh no—I think you disliked her very much. That was very plain to see."

Linda said:

" Perhaps I didn't like her very much. But one can't say that when a person is dead. It wouldn't be decent."

Poirot sighed. He said:

" They taught you that at your school?"

" More or less, I suppose."

Hercule Poirot said:

" When a person has been murdered, it is more important to be truthful than to be decent."

Linda said:

" I suppose you *would* say a thing like that."

" I would say it and I do say it. It is my business, you see, to find out who killed Arlena Marshall."

Linda muttered:

" I want to forget it all. It's so horrible."

Poirot said gently:

" *But you can't forget, can you?*"

Linda said:

" I suppose some beastly madman killed her."

Hercule Poirot murmured:

" No, I do not think it was quite like that."

Linda caught her breath. She said:

" You sound—as though you *knew?*"

Poirot said:

" Perhaps I do know." He paused and went on, " Will you trust me, my child, to do the best I can for you in your bitter trouble?"

Linda sprang up. She said:

" I haven't any trouble. There is nothing you can do for me. I don't know what you are talking about."

Poirot said, watching her:

" I am talking about *candles . . .*"

He saw the terror leap into her eyes. She cried:

" I won't listen to you. I won't listen."

She ran across the beach, swift as a young gazelle and went flying up the zigzag path.

Poirot shook his head. He looked grave and troubled.

Chapter Eleven

1

INSPECTOR COLGATE was reporting to the Chief Constable.

"I've got on to one thing, sir, and something pretty sensational. It's about Mrs. Marshall's money. I've been into it with her lawyers. I'd say it's a bit of a shock to them. I've got proof of the blackmail story. You remember she was left fifty thousand pounds by old Erskine? Well, all that's left of that is about fifteen thousand."

The Chief Constable whistled.

"Whew, what's become of the rest?"

"That's the interesting point, sir. She's sold out stuff from time to time, and each time she's handled it in cash or negotiable securities—that's to say she's handed out money to someone that she didn't want traced. Blackmail all right."

The Chief Constable nodded.

"Certainly looks like it. And the blackmailer is here in this hotel. That means it must be one of those three men. Got anything fresh on any of them?"

"Can't say I've got anything definite, sir. Major Barry's a retired Army man, as he says. Lives in a small flat, has a pension and a small income from stocks. *But* he's paid in pretty considerable sums into his account in the last year."

"That sounds promising. What's his explanation?"

"Says they're betting gains. It's perfectly true that he goes to all the large race meetings. Places his bets on the course too, doesn't run an account."

The Chief Constable nodded.

"Hard to disprove that," he said. "But it's suggestive."

Colgate went on.

"Next, the Reverend Stephen Lane. He's *bona fide* all right—had a living at St. Helen's, Whiteridge, Surrey—resigned his living just over a year ago owing to ill-health. His ill-health amounted to his going into a nursing home for mental patients. He was there for over a year."

"Interesting," said Weston.

"Yes, sir. I tried to get as much as I could out of the doctor

153

in charge but you know what these medicos are—it's difficult to pin them down to anything you can get hold of. But as far as I can make out, his reverence's trouble was an obsession about the devil—especially the devil in the guise of a woman—scarlet woman—whore of Babylon."

"H'm," said Weston. "There have been precedents for murder there."

"Yes, sir. It seems to me that Stephen Lane is at least a possibility. The late Mrs. Marshall was a pretty good example of what a clergyman would call a Scarlet Woman—hair and goings on an all. Seems to me it's not impossible he may have felt it his appointed task to dispose of her. That is if he is really batty."

"Nothing to fit in with the blackmail theory?"

"No, sir, I think we can wash him out as far as that's concerned. Has some private means of his own, but not very much, and no sudden increase lately."

"What about his story of his movements on the day of the crime?"

"Can't get any confirmation of them. Nobody remembers meeting a parson in the lanes. As to the book at the church, the last entry was three days before and nobody had looked at it for about a fortnight. He could have quite easily gone over the day before, say, or even a couple of days before, and dated his entry the 25th."

Weston nodded. He said:

"And the third man?"

"Horace Blatt? It's my opinion, sir, that there's definitely something fishy there. Pays income-tax on a sum far exceeding what he makes out of his hardware business. And mind you, he's a slippery customer. He could probably cook up a reasonable statement—he gambles a bit on the Stock Exchange, and he's in with one or two shady deals. Oh, yes, there may be plausible explanations, but there's no getting away from it that he's been making pretty big sums from unexplained sources for some years now."

"In fact," said Weston, "the idea is that Mr. Horace Blatt is a successful blackmailer by profession?"

"Either that, sir, or it's dope. I saw Chief Inspector Ridgeway who's in charge of the dope business, and he was no end keen. Seems there's been a good bit of heroin coming in lately. They're on to the small distributors, and they know more or less who's running it the other end, but it's the way it's coming into the country that's baffled them so far."

Weston said:

"If the Marshall woman's death is the result of her getting mixed up, innocently or otherwise, with the dope-running stunt, then we'd better hand the whole thing over to Scotland Yard. It's their pigeon. Eh? What do you say?"

Inspector Colgate said rather regretfully:

"I'm afraid you're right, sir. If it's dope, then it's a case for the Yard."

Weston said after a moment or two's thought:

"It really seems the most likely explanation."

Colgate nodded gloomily.

"Yes, it does. Marshall's right out of it—though I did get some information that might have been useful if his alibi hadn't been so good. Seems his firm is very near the rocks. Not his fault or his partner's, just the general result of the crisis last year and the general state of trade and finance. And as far as he knew, he'd come into fifty thousand pounds if his wife died. And fifty thousand would have been a very useful sum."

He sighed.

"Seems a pity when a man's got two perfectly good motives for murder, that he can be proved to have had nothing to do with it!"

Weston smiled.

"Cheer up, Colgate. There's still a chance we may distinguish ourselves. There's the blackmail angle still and there's the batty parson, but, personally, I think the dope solution is far the most likely." He added: "And if it was one of the dope gang who put her out we'll have been instrumental in helping Scotland Yard to solve the dope problem. In fact, take it all round, one way or another, we've done pretty well."

An unwilling smile showed on Colgate's face.

He said:

"Well, that's the lot, sir. By the way, I checked up on the writer of that letter we found in her room. The one signed J.N. Nothing doing. He's in China safe enough. Same chap as Miss Brewster was telling us about. Bit of a young scallywag. I've checked up on the rest of Mrs. Marshall's friends. No leads there. Everything there is to get, we've got, sir."

Weston said:

" So now it's up to us." He paused and then added: " Seen anything of out Belgian colleague? Does he know all you've told me?"

Colgate said with a grin.

" He's a queer little cuss, isn't he? D'you know what he asked me day before yesterday? He wanted particulars of any cases of strangulation in the last three years."

Colonel Weston sat up.

" He did, did he? Now I wonder——" he paused a minute. " When did you say the Reverend Stephen Lane went into that mental home?"

" A year ago last Easter, sir."

Colonel Weston was thinking deeply. He said:

" There was a case—body of a young woman found somewhere near Bagshot. Going to meet her husband somewhere and never turned up. And there was what the papers called the Lonely Copse Mystery. Both in Surrey if I remember rightly."

His eyes met those of his Inspector. Colgate said:

" Surrey? My word, sir, it fits, doesn't it? I wonder ..."

2

Hercule Poirot sat on the turf on the summit of the island.

A little to his left was the beginning of the steel ladder that led down to Pixy's Cove. There were several rough boulders near the head of the ladder, he noted, forming easy concealment for any one who proposed to descend to the beach below. Of the beach itself little could be seen from the top owing to the overhang of the cliff.

Hercule Poirot nodded his head gravely.

The pieces of his jig-saw were fitting into position.

Mentally he went over those pieces, considering each as a detached item.

A morning on the bathing beach some few days before Arlena Marshall's death.

One, two, three, four, five separate remarks uttered on that morning.

The evening of a bridge game. He, Patrick Redfern and Rosamund Darnley had been at the table. Christine had wandered out while dummy and had overheard a certain conversation. Who else had been in the lounge at that time? Who had been absent?

The evening before the crime. The conversation he had had with Christine on the cliff and the scene he had witnessed on his way back to the hotel.

Gabrielle No. 8.

A pair of scissors.

A broken pipe stem.

A bottle thrown from a window.

A green calendar.

A packet of candles.

A mirror and a typewriter.

A skein of magenta wool.

A girl's wrist-watch.

Bathwater rushing down the waste-pipe.

Each of these unrelated facts must fit into its appointed place. There must be no loose ends.

And then, with each concrete fact fitted into position, on to the next step: his own belief in the presence of evil on the island.

Evil. . . .

He looked down at a typewritten paper in his hands.

Nellie Parsons—found strangled in a lonely copse near Chobham. No clue to her murderer ever discovered.

Nellie Parsons?

Alice Corrigan.

He read very carefully the details of Alice Corrigan's death.

3

To Hercule Poirot, sitting on the ledge overlooking the sea, came Inspector Colgate.

Poirot liked Inspector Colgate. He liked his rugged face, his shrewd eyes, and his slow unhurried manner.

Inspector Colgate sat down. He said, glancing down at the typewritten sheets in Poirot's hand:

" Done anything with those cases, sir?"

" I have studied them—yes."

Colgate got up, he walked along and peered into the next niche. He came back, saying:

" One can't be too careful. Don't want to be overheard."

Poirot said:

" You are wise."

Colgate said:

" I don't mind telling you, M. Poirot, that I've been interested in those cases myself—though perhaps I shouldn't have thought about them if you hadn't asked for them." He paused. " I've been interested in one case in particular."

" Alice Corrigan?"

" Alice Corrigan." He paused. " I've been on to the Surrey police about that case—wanted to get all the ins and outs of it."

" Tell me, my friend. I am interested—very interested."

" I thought you might be. Alice Corrigan was found strangled in Cæsar's Grove on Blackridge Heath—not ten miles from Marley Copse where Nellie Parsons was found— and both those places are within twelve miles of Whiteridge where Mr. Lane was vicar."

Poirot said:

" Tell me more about the death of Alice Corrigan."

Colgate said:

" The Surrey police didn't at first connect her death with that of Nellie Parsons. That's because they'd pitched on the husband as the guilty party. Don't quite know why except that he was a bit of what the Press calls a ' mystery man '—not much known about him—who he was or where he came from. She'd married him against her people's wishes, she'd a bit of money of her own—and she'd insured her life in his favour—all that was enough to raise suspicion, as I think you'll agree, sir?"

Poirot nodded.

" But when it came down to brass tacks the husband was washed right out of the picture. The body was discovered by one of these women hikers—hefty young women in shorts. She was an absolutely competent and reliable witness—games mistress at a school in Lancashire. She noted the time when she found the body—it was exactly four-fifteen—and gave it as her opinion that the woman had been dead quite a short time—not more than ten minutes. That fitted in well enough with the police surgeon's view when he examined the body at 5.45. She left everything as it was and tramped across country to Bagshot police station where she reported the death. Now from three o'clock to four-ten, Edward Corrigan was in the train coming down from London where he'd gone up for the day on business. Four other people were in the carriage with him. From the station he took the local bus, two of his fellow passengers travelling by it also. He got off at the Pine Ridge Café where he'd arranged to meet his wife for tea. Time then was four twenty-five. He ordered tea for them both, but said not to bring it till she came. Then he walked about outside waiting for her. When, by five o'clock she hadn't turned up, he was getting alarmed—thought she might have sprained her ankle. The arrangement was that she was to walk across the moors from the village where they were staying to the Pine Ridge Café and go home by bus. Cæsar's Grove is not far from the café, and it's thought that as she was ahead of time she sat down there to admire the view for a bit before going on, and that some tramp or madman came upon her there and caught her unawares. Once the husband was proved to be out of it, naturally they connected up her death with that of Nellie Parsons—that rather flighty servant girl who was found strangled in Marley Copse. They decided that the same man was responsible for both crimes, but they never caught him—and what's more they never came near to catching him! Drew a blank everywhere."

He paused and then he said slowly:

"And now—here's a third woman strangled—and a certain gentleman we won't name right on the spot."

He stopped.

His small shrewd eyes came round to Poirot. He waited hopefully.

Poirot's lips moved. Inspector Colgate leaned forward.

Poirot was murmuring:

"—— so difficult to know which pieces are part of the fur rug and which are the cat's tail."

"I *beg* pardon, sir?" said Inspector Colgate, startled.

Poirot said quickly.

"I apologise. I was following a train of thought of my own. What's this about a fur rug and a cat?"

"Nothing—nothing at all." He paused. "Tell me, Inspector Colgate, if you suspected someone of telling lies—

many, many lies but you had no proof, what would you do?"

Inspector Colgate considered.

" It's difficult, that is. But it's my opinion that if any one tells enough lies, they're bound to trip up in the end."

Poirot nodded.

" Yes, that is very true. You see, it is only in my mind that certain statements are lies. I *think* that they are lies, but I cannot *know* that they are lies. But one might perhaps make a test—a test of one little not very noticeable lie. And if that were proved to be a lie—why then, one would know that all the rest were lies, too!"

Inspector Colgate looked at him curiously.

" Your mind works a funny way, doesn't it, sir? But I dare say it comes out all right in the end. If you'll excuse me asking, what put you on to asking about strangulation cases in general?"

Poirot said slowly:

" You have a word in your language—*slick*. This crime seemed to me a very slick crime! It made me wonder if, perhaps, it was not a first attempt."

Inspector Colgate said:

" I see."

Poirot went on:

" I said to myself, let us examine past crimes of a similar kind and if there is a crime that closely resembles this one— *eh bien*, we shall have there a very valuable clue."

" You mean using the same method of death, sir?"

" No, no, I mean more than that. The death of Nellie Parsons for instance tells me nothing. But the death of Alice Corrigan—tell me, Inspector Colgate, do you not notice one striking form of similarity in this crime?"

Inspector Colgate turned the problem over in his mind. He said at last.

" No, sir, I can't say that I do really. Unless it's that in each case the husband has got a cast-iron alibi."

Poirot said softly:

" Ah, so you *have* noticed that?"

4

" Ha, Poirot. Glad to see you. Come in. Just the man I want."

Hercult Poirot responded to the invitation.

The Chief Constable pushed over a box of cigarettes, took one himself and lighted it. Between puffs he said:

" I've decided, more or less, on a course of action. But I'd like your opinion on it before I act decisively."

Hercule Poirot said:

" Tell me, my friend."

Weston said:

" I've decided to call in Scotland Yard and hand the case over to them. In my opinion, although there have been grounds for suspicion against one or two people, the whole case hinges on dope smuggling. It seems clear to me that that place, Pixy's Cave, was a definite rendezvous for the stuff."

Poirot nodded.

" I agree."

" Good man. And I'm pretty certain who our dope smuggler is. Horace Blatt."

Again Poirot assented. He said:

" That, too, is indicated."

" I see our minds have both worked the same way. Blatt used to go sailing in that boat of his. Sometimes he'd invite people to go with him, but most of the time he went out alone. He had some rather conspicuous red sails on that boat, but we've found that he had some white sails as well stowed away. I think he sailed out on a good day to an appointed spot, and was met by another boat—sailing boat or motor yacht— something of the kind and the stuff was handed over. Then Blatt would run ashore into Pixy's Cove at a suitable time of day——"

Hercule Poirot smiled:

" Yes, yes, at half-past one. The hour of the British lunch when every one is quite sure to be in the dining-room. The island is private. It is not a place where outsiders come for picnics. People take their tea sometimes from the hotel to Pixy's Cove in the afternoon when the sun is on it, or

F

if they want a picnic they would go somewhere far afield, many miles away."

The Chief Constable nodded.

"Quite," he said. "Therefore, Blatt ran ashore there and stowed the stuff on that ledge in the cave. Somebody else was to pick it up there in due course."

Poirot murmured:

"There was a couple, you remember, who came to the island for lunch on the day of the murder? That would be a way of getting the stuff. Some summer visitors from a hotel on the Moor or at St. Loo come over to Smugglers' Island. They announce that they will have lunch. They walk round the island first. How easy to descend to the beach, pick up the sandwich box, place it, no doubt, in Madame's bathing-bag which she carries—and return for lunch to the hotel—a little late, perhaps, say at ten minutes to two, having enjoyed their walk whilst every one else was in the dining-room."

Weston said:

"Yes, it all sounds practicable enough. Now these dope organisations are pretty ruthless. If any one blundered in and got wise to things they wouldn't make any bones about silencing that person. It seems to me that that is the right explanation of Arlena Marshall's death. It's possible that on that morning Blatt was actually at the cove stowing the stuff away. His accomplices were to come for it that very day. Arlena arrives on her float and sees him going into the cave with the box. She asks him about it and he kills her then and there and sheers off in his boat as quick as possible."

Poirot said:

"You think definitely that Blatt is the murderer?"

"It seems the most probable solution. Of course it's possible that Arlena might have got on to the truth earlier, said something to Blatt about it, and some other member of the gang fixed a fake appointment with her and did her in. As I say, I think the best course is to hand the case over to Scotland Yard. They've a far better chance than we have of proving Blatt's connection with the gang."

Hercule Poirot nodded thoughtfully.

Weston said:

"You think that's the wise thing to do—eh?"

Poirot was thoughtful. He said at last: "It may be."

" Dash it all, Poirot, have you got something up your sleeve, or haven't you?"

Poirt said gravely:

" If I have, I am not sure that I can prove it."

Weston said:

" Of course, I know that you and Colgate have other ideas. Seems a bit fantastic to me, but I'm bound to admit there may be something in it. But even if you're right. I still think it's a case for the Yard. We'll give them the facts and they can work in with the Surrey police. What I feel is that it isn't really a case for us. It's not sufficiently localised."

He paused.

" What do you think, Poirot? What do you feel ought to be done about it?"

Poirot seemed lost in thought. At last he said:

" I know what I should like to do."

" Yes, man."

Poirot murmured:

" I should like to go for a picnic."

Colonel Weston stared at him.

Chapter Twelve

1

" A picnic, M. Poirot?"

Emily Brewster stared at him as though he were out of his senses.

Poirot said engagingly:

" It sounds to you, does it not, very outrageous? But indeed it seems to me a most admirable idea. We need something of the every day, the usual, to restore life to the normal. I am most anxious to see something of Dartmoor, the weather is good. It will—how shall I say, it will cheer everybody up! So aid me in this matter. Persuade every one."

The idea met with unexpected success. Every one was at first dubious and then grudgingly admitted it might not be such a bad idea after all.

It was not suggested that Captain Marshall should be asked.

He had himself announced that he had to go to Plymouth that day. Mr. Blatt was of the party, enthusiastically so. He was determined to be the life and soul of it. Besides him there was Emily Brewster, the Redferns, Stephen Lane, the Gardeners, who were persuaded to delay their departure by one day, Rosamund Darnley and Linda.

Poirot had been eloquent to Rosamund and had dwelt on the advantage it would be to Linda to have something to take her out of herself. To this Rosamund agreed. She said:

"You're quite right. The shock has been very bad for a child of that age. It has made her terribly jumpy."

"That is only natural, Mademoiselle. But at that age one soon forgets. Persuade her to come. You can, I know."

Major Barry had refused firmly. He said he didn't like picnics. "Lots of baskets to carry," he said. "And darned uncomfortable. Eating my food at a table's good enough for me."

The party assembled at ten o'clock. Three cars had been ordered. Mr. Blatt was loud and cheerful, imitating a tourist guide.

"This way, ladies and gentlemen—this way for Dartmoor. Heather and bilberries, Devonshire cream and convicts. Bring your wives, gentlemen, or bring the other thing! Every one welcome! Scenery guaranteed. Walk up. Walk up."

At the last minute Rosamund Darnley came down looking concerned. She said:

"Linda's not coming. She says she's got a frightful headache."

Poirot cried:

"But it will do her good to come. Persuade her, Mademoiselle."

Rosamund said firmly:

"It's no good. She's absolutely determined. I've given her some aspirin and she's gone to bed."

She hesitated and said:

"I think, perhaps, I won't go, either."

"Can't allow that, dear lady, can't allow that," cried Mr. Blatt, seizing her facetiously by the arm. " *La haute Mode* must grace the occasion. No refusals! I've taken you into custody, ha, ha. Sentenced to Dartmoor."

He led her firmly to the first car. Rosamund threw a black look at Hercule Poirot.

"I'll stay with Linda," said Christine Redfern. "I don't mind a bit."

Patrick said: "Oh, come on, Christine."

And Poirot said:

"No, no, you must come, Madame. With a headache one is better alone. Come, let us start."

The three cars drove off. They went first to the real Pixy's Cave on Sheepstor, and had a good deal of fun looking for the entrance and at last finding it, aided by a picture postcard.

It was precarious going on the big boulders and Hercule Poirot did not attempt it. He watched indulgently while Christine Redfern sprang lightly from stone to stone and observed that her husband was never far from her. Rosamund Darnley and Emily Brewster had joined in the search though the latter slipped once and gave a slight twist to her ankle. Stephen Lane was indefatigable, his long lean figure turning and twisting among the boulders. Mr. Blatt contented himself with going a little way and shouting encouragement, also taking photographs of the searchers.

The Gardeners and Poirot remained staidly sitting by the wayside whilst Mrs. Gardener's voice upraised itself in a pleasant even-toned monologue, punctuated now and then by the obedient "Yes, darlings" of her spouse.

"——and what I always have felt, M. Poirot, and Mr. Gardener agrees with me, is that snapshots can be very annoying. Unless, that is to say, they are taken among friends. That Mr. Blatt has just no sensitiveness of any kind. He just comes right up to every one and talks away and takes pictures of you and, as I said to Mr. Gardener, that really is very ill-bred. That's what I said, Odell, wasn't it?"

"Yes, darling."

"That group he took of us all sitting on the beach. Well, that's all very well, but he should have asked first. As it was, Miss Brewster was just getting up from the beach, and it certainly makes her look a very peculiar shape."

"I'll say it does," said Mr. Gardener with a grin.

"And there's Mr. Blatt giving round copies to everybody without so much as asking first. He gave one to you, M. Poirot, I noticed."

Poirot nodded. He said:

" I value that group very much."

Mrs. Gardener went on:

" And look at his behaviour to-day—so loud and noisy and common. Why, it just makes me shudder. You ought to have arranged to leave that man at home, M. Poirot."

Hercule Poirot murmured:

" Alas, Madame, that would have been difficult."

" I should say it would. That man just pushes his way in anywhere. He's just not sensitive at all."

At this moment the discovery of the Pixy's Cave was hailed from below with loud cries.

The party now drove on, under Hercule Poirot's directions, to a spot where a short walk from the car down a hillside of heather led to a delightful spot by a small river.

A narrow plank bridge crossed the river and Poirot and her husband induced Mrs. Gardener to cross it to where a delightful heathery spot free from prickly furze looked an ideal spot for a picnic lunch.

Talking volubly about her sensations when crossing on a plank bridge Mrs. Gardener sank down. Suddenly there was a slight outcry.

The others had run across the bridge lightly enough, but Emily Brewster was standing in the middle of the plank, her eyes shut, swaying to and fro.

Poirot and Patrick Redfern rushed to the rescue.

Emily Brewster was gruff and ashamed.

" Thanks, thanks. Sorry. Never was good at crossing running water. Get giddy. Stupid, very."

Lunch was spread out and the picnic began.

All the people concerned were secretly surprised to find how much they enjoyed this interlude. It was, perhaps, because it afforded an escape from an atmosphere of suspicion and dread. Here, with the trickling of the water, the soft peaty smell in the air and the warm colouring of bracken and heather, a world of murder and police inquiries and suspicion seemed blotted out as though it had never existed. Even Mr. Blatt forgot to be the life and soul of the party. After lunch he went to sleep a little distance away and subdued snores testified to his blissful unconsciousness.

It was quite a grateful party of people who packed up the

picnic baskets and congratulated Hercule Poirot on his good idea.

The sun was sinking as they returned along the narrow winding lanes. From the top of the hill above Leathercombe Bay they had a brief glimpse of the island with the white hotel on it.

It looked peaceful and innocent in the setting sun.

Mrs. Gardener, not loquacious for once, sighed and said:

"I really do thank you, M. Poirot. I feel so calm. It's just wonderful."

2

Major Barry came out to greet them on arrival.

"Hullo," he said. "Had a good day?"

Mrs. Gardener said:

"Indeed we did. The moors were just too lovely for anything. So English and old world. And the air delicious and invigorating. You ought to be ashamed of yourself for being so lazy as to stay behind."

The Major chuckled.

"I'm to old for that kind of thing—sitting on a patch of bog and eating sandwiches."

A chambermaid had come out of the hotel. She was a little out of breath. She hesitated for a moment then came swiftly up to Christine Redfern.

Hercule Poirot recognised her as Gladys Narracott. Her voice came quick and uneven.

"Excuse me, Madam, but I'm worried about the young lady. About Miss Marshall. I took her up some tea just now and I couldn't get her to wake, and she looks so—so queer somehow."

Christine looked round helplessly. Poirot was at her side in a moment. His hand under her elbow he said quietly:

"We will go up and see."

They hurried up the stairs and along the passage to Linda's room.

One glance at her was enough to tell them both that something was very wrong. She was an odd colour and her breathing was hardly perceptible.

Poirot's hand went to her pulse. At the same time he noticed an envelope stuck up against the lamp on the bedside table. It was addressed to himself.

Captain Marshall came quickly into the room. He said:

"What's this about Linda? What's the matter with her?"

A small frightened sob came from Christine Redfern.

Hercule Poirot turned from the bed. He said to Marshall.

"Get a doctor—as quick as you possibly can. But I'm afraid—very much afraid—it may be too late."

He took the letter with his name on it and ripped open the envelope Inside were a few lines of writing in Linda's prim schoolgirl hand.

I think this is the best way out. Ask Father to try and forgive me. I killed Arlena. I thought I should be glad—but I'm not. I am very sorry for everything.

3

They were assembled in the lounge—Marshall, the Redferns, Rosamund Darnley and Hercule Poirot.

They sat there silent—waiting. . . .

The door opened and Dr. Neasdon came in. He said curtly:

"I've done all I can. She may pull through—but I'm bound to tell you that there's not much hope."

He paused. Marshall, his face stiff, his eyes a cold frosty blue asked:

"How did she get hold of the stuff?"

Neasdon opened the door again and beckoned.

The chambermaid came into the room. She had been crying:

Neasdon said:

"Just tell us again what you saw?"

Sniffing, the girl said:

"I never thought—I never thought for a minute there was anything wrong—though the young lady did seem rather strange about it." A slight gesture of impatience from the doctor started her off again. "She was in the other lady's room. Mrs. Redfern's. Your room, Madam. Over at the washstand, and she took up a little bottle. She did give a bit of a jump when I came in, and I thought it was queer her taking things from your room, but then, of course, it might be something she'd lent you. She just said: ' Oh, this is what I'm looking for——' and went out."

Christine said almost in a whisper.

" My sleeping tablets."

The doctor said brusquely:

" How did she know about them?"

Christine said:

" I gave her one. The night after it happened. She told me she couldn't sleep. She—I remember her saying—' Will one be enough?'—and I said, Oh yes, they were very strong—that I'd been cautioned never to take more than two at most."

Neasdon nodded. " She made pretty sure," he said. " Took six of them."

Christine sobbed again.

" Oh dear, I feel it's my fault. I should have kept them locked up."

The doctor shrugged his shoulders.

" It might have been wiser, Mrs. Redfern."

Christine said despairingly:

" She's dying—and it's my fault . . ."

Kenneth Marshall stirred in his chair. He said:

" No, you can't blame yourself. Linda knew what she was doing. She took them deliberately. Perhaps—perhaps it was best."

He looked down at the crumpled note in his hand—the note that Poirot had silently handed to him.

Rosamund Darnley cried out.

" I don't believe it. I don't believe Linda killed her. Surely it's impossible—on the evidence!"

Christine said eagerly:

" Yes, she *can't* have done it! She must have got over-wrought and imagined it all."

The door opened and Colonel Weston came in. He said:

" What's all this I hear?"

Dr. Neasdon took the note from Marshall's hand and handed it to the Chief Constable. The latter read it. He exclaimed incredulously:

" What? But this is nonsense—absolute nonsense! It's impossible." He repeated with assurance. " Impossible! Isn't it, Poirot?"

Hercule Poirot moved for the first time. He said in a slow sad voice:

" No, I'm afraid it is not impossible."

Christine Redfern said:

" But I was with her, M. Poirot. I was with her up to a quarter to twelve. I told the police so."

Poirot said:

" Your evidence gave her an alibi—yes. But what was your evidence based on? It was based on *Linda Marshall's own wrist-watch*. You do not know *of your own knowledge* that it was a quarter to twelve when you left her—you only know that she told you so. You said yourself the time seemed to have gone very fast."

She stared at him, stricken.

He said:

" Now think, Madame, when you left the beach, did you walk back to the hotel fast or slow?"

" I—well, fairly slowly, I think."

" Do you remember much about that walk back?"

" Not very much, I'm afraid. I—I was thinking."

Poirot said:

" I am sorry to ask you this, but will you tell just what you were thinking about during that walk?"

Christine flushed.

" I suppose—if it is necessary . . . I was considering the question of—of leaving here. Just going away without telling my husband. I—I was very unhappy just then, you see."

Patrick Redfern cried:

" Oh, Christine! I know . . . I know . . ."

Poirot's precise voice cut in.

" Exactly. You were concerned over taking a step of some importance. You were, I should say, deaf and blind to your surroundings. You probably walked very slowly and occasionally stopped for some minutes whilst you puzzled things out."

Christine nodded.

" How clever you are. It was just like that. I woke up from a kind of dream just outside the hotel and hurried in thinking I should be very late, but when I saw the clock in the lounge I realised I had plenty of time."

Hercule Poirot said again:

" Exactly."

He turned to Marshall.

" I must now describe to you certain things I found in your

daughter's room after the murder. In the grate was a large blob of melted wax, some burnt hair, fragments of cardboard and paper and an ordinary household pin. The paper and the cardboard might not be relevant, but the other three things were suggestive—particularly when I found tucked away in the bookshelf a volume from the local library here dealing with witchcraft and magic. It opened very easily at a certain page. On that page were described various methods of causing death by moulding in wax a figure supposed to represent the victim. This was then slowly roasted till it melted away—or alternatively you would pierce the wax figure to the heart with a pin. Death of the victim would ensue. I later heard from Mrs. Redfern that Linda Marshall had been out early that morning and had bought a packet of candles, and had seemed embarrassed when her purchase was revealed. I had no doubt what had happened after that. Linda had made a crude figure of the candle wax—possibly adorning it with a snip of Arlena's red hair to give the magic force—had then stabbed it to the heart with a pin and finally melted the figure away by lighting strips of cardboard under it.

" It was crude, childish, superstitious, but it revealed one thing: the desire to kill.

" Was there any possibility that there had been more than a desire? Could Linda Marshall have *actually* killed her stepmother?

" At first sight it seemed as though she had a perfect alibi—but in actuality, as I have just pointed out, the time evidence was supplied *by Linda herself*. She could easily have declared the time to be a quarter of an hour later than it really was.

" It was quite possible once Mrs. Redfern had left the beach for Linda to follow her up and then strike across the narrow neck of land to the ladder, hurry down it, meet her stepmother there, strangle her and return up the ladder before the boat containing Miss Brewster and Patrick Redfern came in sight. She could then return to Gull Cove, take her bathe and return to the hotel at her leisure.

" But that entailed two things. She must have definite knowledge that Arlena Marshall would be at Pixy Cove and she must be physically capable of the deed.

" Well the first was quite possible—if Linda Marshall had written a note to Arlena herself in someone else's name. As to the second, Linda has very large strong hands. They are as large as a man's. As to the strength, she is at the age when one is prone to be mentally unbalanced. Mental derangement often is accompanied by unusual strength. There was one other small point. Linda Marshall's mother had actually been accused and tried for murder."

Kenneth Marshall lifted his head. He said fiercely: " She was also acquitted."

" She was acquitted," Poirot agreed.

Marshall said:

" And I'll tell you this, M. Poirot. Ruth—my wife— was innocent. That I know with complete and absolute certainty. In the intimacy of our life I could not have been deceived. She was an innocent victim of circumstances."

He paused.

" And I don't believe that Linda killed Arlena. It's ridiculous—absurd!"

Poirot said:

" Do you believe that letter, then, to be a forgery?"

Marshall held out his hand for it and Weston gave it to him. Marshall studied it attentively. Then he shook his head.

" No," he said unwillingly. " I believe Linda did write this."

Poirot said:

" Then if she wrote it, there are only two explanations. Either she wrote it in all good faith, knowing herself to be the murderess or—or, I say—*she wrote it deliberately to shield someone else,* someone whom she feared was suspected."

Kenneth Marshall said:

" You mean me?"

" It is possible, is it not?"

Marshall considered for a moment or two, then he said quietly:

" No, I think that idea is absurd. Linda may have realised that I was regarded with suspicion at first. But she knew definitely by now that that was over and done with—that the police had accepted my alibi and turned their attention elsewhere."

Poirot said:

" And supposing that it was not so much that she thought that you were suspected as that she *knew* you were guilty."

Marshall stared at him. He gave a short laugh.

" That's absurd."

Poirot said:

" I wonder. There are, you know, several possibilities about Mrs. Marshall's death. There is the theory that she was being blackmailed, that she went that morning to meet the blackmailer and that the blackmailer killed her. There is the theory that Pixy Cove and Cave were being used for drug-running, and that she was killed because she accidentally learned something about that. There is a third possibility—that she was killed by a religious maniac. And there is a fourth possibility—you stood to gain a lot of money by your wife's death, Captain Marshall?"

" I've just told you——"

" Yes, yes—I agree that it is impossible that you could have killed your wife—*if you were acting alone*. But supposing someone helped you?"

" What the devil do you mean?"

The quiet man was roused at last. He half rose from his chair. His voice was menacing. There was a hard angry light in his eyes.

Poirot said:

" I mean that this is not a crime that was committed single-handed. Two people were in it. It is quite true that you could not have typed that letter and at the same time gone to the cove—but there would have been time for you to have jotted down that letter in shorthand—and for *someone else* to have typed it in your room while you yourself were absent on your murderous errand."

Hercule Poirot looked towards Rosamund Darnley. He said:

" Miss Darnley states that she left Sunny Ledge at ten minutes past eleven and saw you typing in your room. But just about that time Mr Gardener went up to the hotel to fetch a skein of wool for his wife. He did not meet Miss Darnley or see her. That is rather remarkable. It looks as though either Miss Darnley never left Sunny Ledge, or else she had left it much earlier and was in your room typing industriously. Another point, you stated that when Miss Darnley looked into your room at a quarter past eleven *you saw her in the mirror*. But on the day of the murder your typewriter and papers were all on the writing-desk across the corner of the room, whereas the mirror was between the windows. So that that statement was a deliberate lie. Later, you moved your typewriter to the table under the mirror so as to substantiate your story—but it was too late. I was aware that both you and Miss Darnley had lied."

Rosamund Darnley spoke. Her voice was low and clear. She said:

"How devilishly ingenious you are!"

Hercule Poirot said, raising his voice:

"But not so devilish and so ingenious as the man who killed Arlena Marshall! Think back for a moment. Who did I think—who did everybody think—that Arlena Marshall had gone to meet that morning? We all jumped to the same conclusion. *Patrick Redfern*. It was not to meet a blackmailer that she went. Her face alone would have told me that. Oh no, it was a lover she was going to meet—or thought she was going to meet.

"Yes, I was quite sure of that. Arlena Marshall was going to meet Patrick Redfern. But a minute later Patrick Redfern appeared on the beach and was obviously looking for her. So what then?"

Patrick Redfern said with subdued anger:

"Some devil used my name."

Poirot said:

"You were very obviously upset and surprised by her non-appearance. Almost too obviously, perhaps. It is *my* theory, Mr. Redfern, that she went to Pixy Cove to meet *you*, and that she *did* meet you, and that *you killed her there as you had planned to do*."

Patrick Redfern stared. He said in his high good-humoured Irish voice:

"Is it daft you are? I was with you on the beach until I went round in the boat with Miss Brewster and found her dead."

Hercule Poirot said:

"You killed her after Miss Brewster had gone off in the boat to fetch the police. Arlena Marshall was not dead when you got to the beach. She was waiting hidden in the cave until the coast should be clear."

"But the body! Miss Brewster and I both saw the body."

"*A* body—yes. But not a *dead* body. The *live* body of the woman who helped you, her arms and legs stained with tan, her face hidden by a green cardboard hat. Christine, your wife (or possibly not your wife—but still your partner),

helping you to commit this crime as she helped you to commit
that crime in the past when she "discovered" the body of
Alice Corrigan at least twenty minutes before Alice
Corrigan died—killed by her husband Edward Corrigan—
you!"

Christine spoke. Her voice was sharp—cold. She said:
"Be careful, Patrick, don't lose your temper."

Poirot said:

"You will be interested to hear that both you and your
wife Christine were easily recognised and picked out by the
Surrey police from a group of people photographed here.
They identified you both at once as Edward Corrigan and
Christine Deverill, the young woman who found the body."

Patrick Redfern had risen. His handsome face was trans-
formed, suffused with blood, blind with rage. It was the face
of a killer—of a tiger. He yelled:

"You damned interfering murdering lousy little worm!"

He hurled himself forward, his fingers stretching and curling,
his voice raving curses, as he fastened his fingers round
Hercule Poirot's throat . . .

Chapter Thirteen

1

POIROT said reflectively:

"It was on a morning when we were sitting out here that
we talked of sun-tanned bodies lying like meat upon a slab,
and it was then that I reflected how little difference there
was between one body and another. If one looked closely
and appraisingly—yes—but to the casual glance? One
moderately well-made young woman is very like another. Two
brown legs, two brown arms, a little piece of bathing suit in
between—just a body lying out in the sun. When a woman
walks, when she speaks, laughs, turns her head, moves a hand
—then, yes then, there is personality—individuality. But in the
sun ritual—no.

"It was that day that we spoke of evil—*evil under the sun*
as Mr. Lane put it. Mr. Lane is a very sensitive person—evil
affects him—he perceives its presence—but though he is a

good recording instrument, he did not really know exactly where the evil was. To him, evil was focused in the person of Arlena Marshall, and practically every one present agreed with him.

"But to my mind, though evil was present, it was not centralised in Arlena Marshall at all. It was connected with her, yes—but in a totally different way. I saw her, first, last and all the time, as an eternal and predestined *victim*. Because she was beautiful, because she had glamour, because men turned their heads to look at her, it was assumed that she was the type of woman who wrecked lives and destroyed souls. But I saw her very differently. It was not she who fatally attracted men—it was men who fatally attracted her. She was the type of woman whom men care for easily and of whom they as easily tire. And everything that I was told or found out about her strengthened my conviction on this point. The first thing that was mentioned about her was how the man in whose divorce case she had been cited refused to marry her. It was then that Captain Marshall, one of those incurably chivalrous men, stepped in and asked her to marry him. To a shy retiring man of Captain Marshall's type, a public ordeal of any kind would be the worst torture—hence his love and pity for his first wife who was publicly accused and tried for a murder she had not committed. He married her and found himself amply justified in his estimate of her character. After her death another beautiful woman, perhaps something of the same type (since Linda has red hair which she probably inherited from her mother), is held up to public ignomiuy. Again Marshall performs a rescue act. But this time he finds little to sustain his infatuation. Arlena is stupid, unworthy of his sympathy and protection, mindless. Nevertheless, I think he always had a fairly true vision of her. Long after he ceased to love her and was irked by her presence, he remained sorry for her. She was to him like a child who cannot get farther than a certain page in the book of life.

"I saw in Arlena Marshall with her passion for men, a predestined prey for an unscrupulous man of a certain type. In Patrick Redfern, with his good looks, his easy assurance, his undeniable charm for women, I recognised at once that type. The adventurer who makes his living, one way or another, out of women. Looking on from my place on the beach I was quite certain that Arlena was Patrick's victim, not the other way about. And I associated that focus of evil with Patrick Redfern, not with Arlena Marshall.

"Arlena had recently come into a large sum of money, left her by an elderly admirer who had not had time to grow tired of her. She was the type of woman who is invariably defrauded of money by some man or other. Miss Brewster mentioned a young man who had been 'ruined' by Arlena, but a letter from him which was found in her room, though it expressed a wish (which cost nothing) to cover her with jewels, in actual *fact* acknowledged a cheque from *her* by means of which he hoped to escape prosecution. A clear case of a young waster sponging on her. I have no doubt that Patrick Redfern found it easy to induce her to hand him large sums from time to time 'for investment.' He probably dazzled her with stories of great opportunities—how he would make her fortune and his own. Unprotected women, living alone, are easy prey to that type of man—and he usually escapes scot free with the booty. If, however, there is a husband, or a brother, or a father about, things are apt to take an unpleasant turn for the swindler. Once Captain Marshall was to find out what had happened to his wife's fortune, Patrick Redfern might expect short shrift.

"That did not worry him, however, because he contemplated quite calmly doing away with her when he judged it necessary —encouraged by having already got away with one murder— that of a young woman whom he had married in the name of Corrigan and whom he had persuaded to insure her life for a large sum.

"In his plans he was aided and abetted by the woman who down here passed as his wife and to whom he was genuinely attached. A young woman as unlike the type of his victims as could well be imagined—cool, calm, passionless, but steadfastly loyal to him and an actress of no mean ability. From the time of her arrival here Christine Redfern played a part, the part of the 'poor little wife'—frail, helpless, intellectual rather than athletic. Think of the points she made one after another. Her tendency to blister in the sun and her consequent white skin, her giddiness at heights—stories of getting stuck on Milan Cathedral, etc. An emphasis on her frailty and delicacy—nearly every one spoke of her as a 'little woman.' She was actually as tall as Arlena Marshall, but with very small hands and feet. She spoke of herself

as a former school-teacher, and thereby emphasised an
impression of book learning and lack of athletic prowess.
Actually it is quite true that she had worked in a school,
but the position she held there was that of *games mistress,* and
she was an extremely active young woman who could climb
like a cat and run like an athlete.

" The crime itself was perfectly planned and timed. It
was, as I mentioned before, a very slick crime. The timing
was a work of genius.

" First of all there were certain preliminary scenes—one
played on the cliff ledge when they knew me to be occupying
the next recess—a conventional jealous wife dialogue between
her and her husband. Later she played the same part in a scene
with me. At the time I remember a vague feeling of having
read all this in a book. It did not seem *real.* Because,
of course, it was *not* real. Then came the day of the crime. It
was a fine day—an essential. Redfern's first act was to slip
out very early—by the balcony door which he unlocked from
the inside (if found open it would only be thought someone
had gone for an early bathe). Under his bathing-wrap he concealed a green Chinese hat, the duplicate of the one Arlena
was in the habit of wearing. He slipped across the island, down
the ladder and stowed it away in an appointed place behind
some rocks. Part I.

" On the previous evening he had arranged a rendezvous
with Arlena. They were exercising a good deal of caution
about meeting as Arlena was slightly afraid of her husband.
She agreed to go round to Pixy Cove early. Nobody went
there in the morning. Redfern was to join her there, taking
a chance to slip away unobtrusively. If she heard any one
descending the ladder or a boat came in sight she was to slip
inside the Pixy's Cave, the secret of which he had told her, and
wait there until the coast was clear. Part II.

" In the meantime Christine went to Linda's room at a
time when she judged Linda would have gone for her early
morning dip. She would then alter Linda's watch, putting it on
twenty minutes. There was, of course, a risk that Linda
might notice her watch was wrong, but it did not much matter
if she did. Christine's real alibi was the size of her hands
which made it a physical impossibility for her to have committed the crime. Nevertheless, an additional alibi would be
desirable. When in Linda's room she noticed the book on

witchcraft and magic, open at a certain page. She read it, and when Linda came in and dropped a parcel of candles she realised what was in Linda's mind. It opened up some new ideas to her. The original idea of the guilty pair had been to cast a reasonable amount of suspicion on Kenneth Marshall, hence the abstracted pipe, a fragment of which was to be planted on the Cove underneath the ladder.

" On Linda's return Christine easily arranged an outing together to Gull Cove. She then returned to her own room, took out from a locked suitcase a bottle of artificial suntan, applied it carefully and threw the empty bottle out of the window where it narrowly escaped hitting Emily Brewster who was bathing. Part III successfully accomplished.

" Christine then dressed herself in a white bathing-suit, and over it a pair of beach trousers and coat with long floppy sleeves which effectually concealed her newly-browned arms and legs.

" At 10.15 Arlena departed for her rendezvous, a minute or two later Patrick Redfern came down and registered surprise, annoyance, etc. Christine's task was easy enough. Keeping her own watch concealed she asked Linda at twenty-five past eleven what time it was. Linda looked at her watch and replied that it was a quarter to twelve. She then starts down to the sea and Christine packs up her sketching things. As soon as Linda's back is turned Christine picks up the girl's watch which she has necessarily discarded before going into the sea and alters it back to the correct time. Then she hurries up the cliff path, runs across the narrow neck of land to the top of the ladder, strips off her pyjamas and shoves them and her sketching box behind a rock and swarms rapidly down the ladder in her best gymnastic fashion.

" Arlena is on the beach below wondering why Patrick is so long in coming. She sees or hears someone on the ladder, takes a cautious observation, and to her annoyance sees that inconvenient person—the wife! She hurries along the beach and into the Pixy's Cave.

Christine takes the hat from its hiding-place, a false red curl pinned underneath the brim at the back, and disposes herself in a sprawling attitude with the hat and curl shielding her face and neck. The timing is perfect. A minute or two later the boat containing Patrick and Emily Brewster comes round the point. Remember it is *Patrick* who bends down and examines the body, *Patrick* who is stunned—shocked—broken down by the death of his lady love! His witness has been carefully chosen. Miss Brewster has not got a good head, she will not attempt to go up the ladder. She will leave the Cove by boat, Patrick naturally being the one to remain with the body—' in case the murderer may be still about.' Miss Brewster rows off to fetch the police. Christine, as soon as the boat has disappeared, springs up, cuts the hat into pieces with the scissors Patrick has carefully brought, stuffs them into her bathing-suit and swarms up the ladder in double quick time, slips into her beach-pyjamas and runs back to the hotel. Just time to have a quick bath, washing off the brown suntan application, and into her tennis dress. One other thing she does. She burns the pieces of the green cardboard hat and the hair in Linda's grate, adding a leaf of a calendar so that it may be associated with the cardboard. Not a *Hat* but a *Calendar* has been burnt. As she suspected, Linda has been experimenting in magic—the blob of wax and the pin shows that.

"Then, down to the tennis court, arriving the last, but showing no signs of flurry or haste.

"And, meanwhile, Patrick has gone to the cave. Arlena has seen nothing and heard very little—a boat—voices—she has prudently remained hidden. But now it is Patrick calling.

"'All clear, darling,' and she comes out, and his hands fasten round her neck—and that is the end of poor foolish beautiful Arlena Marshall . . ."

His voice died away.

For a moment there was silence, then Rosamund Darnley said with a little shiver:

"Yes, you make one see it all. But that's the story from the other side. You haven't told us how *you* came to get at the truth?"

Hercule Poirot said:

"I told you once that I had a very simple mind. Always, from the beginning, it seemed to me that *the most likely person* had killed Arlena Marshall. And the most likely person was Patrick Redfern. He was the type, *par excellence* —the type of the man who exploits women like her—and the type of the killer—the kind of man who will take a woman's savings and cut her throat into the bargain. Who was Arlena going to meet that morning? By the evidence of her face, her smile, her manner, her words to me—*Patrick Redfern*. And therefore, in the very nature of things, it should be Patrick Redfern who killed her.

"But at once I came up, as I told you, against impossibility. Patrick Redfern could not have killed her since he was on the beach and in Miss Brewster's company until the actual discovery of the body. So I looked about for other solutions—and there were several. She could have been killed by her husband—with Miss Darnley's connivance. (They too had both lied as to one point which looked suspicious.) She could have been killed as a result of her having stumbled on the secret of the dope smuggling. She could have been killed, as I said, by a religious maniac, and she could have been killed by her stepdaughter. The latter seemed to me at one time to be the real solution. Linda's manner in her very first interview with the police was significant. An interview that I had with her later assured me of one point. Linda considered herself guilty."

"You mean she imagined that she had actually killed Arlena?"

Rosamund's voice was incredulous.

Hercule Poirot nodded.

"Yes. Remember—she is really little more than a child. She read that book on witchcraft and she half believed it. She hated Arlena. She deliberately made the wax doll, cast her spell, pierced it to the heart, melted it away—*and that very day Arlena dies.* Older and wiser people than Linda have believed fervently in magic. Naturally, she believed that it was all true —that by using magic she had killed her stepmother."

Rosamund cried:

"Oh, poor child, poor child. And I thought—I imagined— something quite different—that she knew something which would——"

Rosamund stopped. Poirot said:

"I know what it was you thought. Actually your manner frightened Linda still further. She believed that her action had really brought about Arlena's death and that you knew it. Christine Redfern worked on her too, introducing the idea of the sleeping tablets to her mind, showing her the way to a speedy and painless expiation of her crime. You see, once Captain Marshall was proved to have an alibi, it was vital for a new suspect to be found. Neither she nor her husband knew about the dope smuggling. They fixed on Linda to be the scapegoat."

Rosamund said:

"What a devil!'"

Poirot nodded.

"Yes, you are right. A cold-blooded and cruel woman. For me, I was in great difficulty. Was Linda guilty only of the childish attempt at witchcraft, or had her hate carried her still further—to the actual act? I tried to get her to confess to me. But it was no good. At that moment I was in grave uncertainty. The Chief Constable was inclined to accept the dope smuggling explanation. I couldn't let it go at that. I went over the facts again very carefully. I had, you see, a collection of jig-saw puzzle pieces, isolated happenings—plain facts. The whole must fit into a complete and harmonious pattern. There were the scissors found on the beach—a bottle thrown from a window—a bath that no one would admit to having taken—all perfectly harmless occurrences in themselves, but rendered significant by the fact that no one would admit to them. Therefore, they *must* be of significance. Nothing about them fitted in with the theories of either Captain Marshall's or Linda's, or of a dope gang's being responsible. And yet they *must* have meaning. I went back again to my first solution—that Patrick Redfern had committed the murder. Was there anything in support of that? Yes, the fact that a very large sum of money was missing from Arlena's account. Who had got that money? Patrick Redfern of course. She was the type of woman easily swindled by a handsome young man—but she was not at all the type of woman to be blackmailed. She was far too transparent, not good enough at keeping a secret. The blackmailer story had never rung true to my mind. And yet there *had* been that conversation overheard—ah, but overheard by whom? *Patrick Redfern's wife.* It was her story—unsupported by any outside evidence. Why was it invented? The answer came to me like lightning. To account for the absence of Arlena's money!

"Patrick and Christine Redfern. The two of them were in it together. Christine hadn't got the physical strength to strangle her or the mental make up. No, it was Patrick who had done it—but that was impossible! Every minute of his time was accounted for until the body was found.

" Body—the word stirred something in my mind—bodies lying on the beach—*all alike*. Patrick Redfern and Emily Brewster had got to the Cove and seen *a body* lying there. A body—suppose it was not Arlena's body but somebody else's? The face was hidden by the great Chinese hat.

" But there *was* only one dead body—Arlena's. Then, could it be—a *live* body—someone pretending to be dead? Could it be Arlena herself, inspired by Patrick to play some kind of a joke. I shook my head—no, too risky. A live body —whose? Was there any woman who would help Redfern? Of course—his wife. But she was a white-skinned delicate creature. Ah yes, but suntan can be applied out of bottles— bottles—a bottle—I had one of my jig-saw pieces. Yes, and afterwards, of course, a bath—to wash that tell-tale stain off before she went out to play tennis. And the scissors? Why, to cut up that duplicate cardboard hat—an unwieldy thing that must be got out of the way, and in the haste the scissors were left behind—the one thing that the pair of murderers forgot.

" But where was Arlena all the time? That again was perfectly clear. Either Rosamund Darnley or Arlena Marshall had been in the Pixy's Cave, the scent they both used told me that. It was certainly not Rosamund Darnley. Then it was Arlena, hiding till the coast should clear.

" When Emily Brewster went off in the boat, Patrick had the beach to himself and full opportunity to commit the crime. Arlena Marshall was killed after a quarter to twelve, but the medical evidence was only concerned with the earliest possible time the crime could have been committed. That Arlena was dead at a quarter to twelve was what was told to the doctor, not what he told the police.

" Two more points had to be settled. Linda Marshall's evidence gave Christine Redfern an alibi. Yes, but that evidence depended on Linda Marshall's wrist-watch. All that was needed was to prove that Christine had had two opportunities of tampering with the watch. I found those easily enough. She had been alone in Linda's room that morning— and there was an indirect proof. Linda was heard to say that she was ' afraid she was going to be late,' but when she got down it was only twenty-five past ten by the lounge clock. The second opportunity was easy—she could alter the watch back again as soon as Linda turned her back and went down to bathe.

"Then there was the question of the ladder. Christine had always declared she had no head for heights. Another carefully prepared lie.

"I had my mosaic now—each piece beautifully fitted into its place. But, unfortunately, I had no definite proof. It was all in my mind.

"It was then that an idea came to me. There was an assurance—a slickness about the crime. I had no doubt that in the future Patrick Redfern would repeat his crime. What about the past? It was remotely possible that this was not his first killing. The method employed, strangulation, was in harmony with his nature—a killer for pleasure as well as for profit. If he was already a murderer I was sure that he would have used the same means. I asked Inspector Colgate for a list of women victims of strangulation. The result filled me with joy. The death of Nellie Parson found strangled in a lonely copse might or might not be Patrick Redfern's work—it might merely have suggested choice of locality to him, but in Alice Corrigan's death I found exactly what I was looking for. In essence the same method. Juggling with time—a murder committed not, as is the usual way, *before* it is supposed to have happened, but *afterwards*. A body supposedly discovered at a quarter past four. A husband with an alibi up to twenty-five past four.

"What really happened? It was said that Edward Corrigan arrived at the Pine Ridge, found his wife not there, *and went out and walked up and down*. Actually, of course, he ran full speed to the rendezvous, Cæsar's Grove (which you will remember was quite nearby), killed her and returned to the café. The girl hiker who reported the crime was a most respectable young lady, games' mistress in a well-known girls' school. Apparently she had no connection with Edward Corrigan. She had to walk some way to report the death. The police surgeon only examined the body at a quarter to six. As in this case the time of death was accepted without question.

"I made one final test. I must know definitely if Mrs. Redfern was a liar. I arranged our little excursion to Dartmoor. If any one has a bad head for heights, they are never comfortable crossing a narrow bridge over running water. Miss Brewster, a genuine sufferer, showed giddiness. But

Christine Redfern, unconcerned, ran across without a qualm. It was a small point, but it was a definite test. If she had told one unnecessary lie—then all the other lies were possible. In the meantime Colgate had got the photograph identified by the Surrey Police. I played my hand in the only way I thought likely to succeed. Having lulled Patrick Redfern into security, I turned on him and did my utmost to make him lose his self-control. The knowledge that he had been identified with Corrigan caused him to lose his head completely."

Hercule Poirot stroked his throat reminiscently.

" What I did," he said with importance, " was exceedingly dangerous—but I do not regret it. I succeeded! I did not suffer in vain."

There was a moment's silence. Then Mrs. Gardener gave a deep sigh.

" Why, M. Poirot," she said. " It's just been too wonderful —hearing just exactly how you got your results. It's every bit as fascinating as a lecture on criminology—in fact it *is* a lecture on criminology. And to think my magenta wool and that sunbathing conversation actually had something to do with it? That really makes me too excited for words, and I'm sure Mr. Gardener feels the same, don't you, Odell?"

" Yes, darling." said Mr. Gardener.

Hercule Poirot said:

" Mr. Gardener too was of assistance to me. I wanted the opinion of a sensible man about Mrs. Marshall. I asked Mr. Gardener what he thought of her."

" Is that so," said Mrs. Gardener. " And what did you say about her, Odell?"

Mr. Gardener coughed. He said:

" Well, darling, I never did think very much of her, you know."

" That's the kind of thing men always say to their wives," said Mrs. Gardener. " And if you ask me, even M. Poirot here is what I should call a shade on the indulgent side about her, calling her a natural victim and all that. Of course it's true that she wasn't a cultured woman at all, and as Captain Marshall isn't here I don't mind saying that she always did seem to me kind of dumb. I said so to Mr. Gardener, didn't I, Odell?"

" Yes, darling," said Mr. Gardener.

2

Linda Marshall sat with Hercule Poirot on Gull Cove. She said:

"Of course I'm glad I didn't die after all. But you know, M. Poirot, it's just the same as if I'd killed her, isn't it? I meant to."

Hercule Poirot said energetically:

"It is not at all the same thing. The wish to kill and the action of killing are two different things. If in your bedroom instead of a little wax figure you had had your stepmother bound and helpless and a dagger in your hand instead of a pin, you would not have pushed it into her heart! Something within you would have said 'no.' It is the same with me. I enrage myself at an imbecile. I say, 'I would like to kick him.' Instead, I kick the table. I say, 'This table, it is the imbecile, I kick him so.' And then, if I have not hurt my toe too much, I feel much better and the table it is not usually damaged. But if the imbecile himself was there I should not kick him. To make the wax figures and stick in the pins, it is silly, yes, it is childish, yes—but it does something useful too. You took the hate out of yourself and put it into that little figure. And with the pin and the fire you destroyed—not your stepmother—but the hate you bore her. Afterwards, even before you heard of her death, you felt cleansed, did you not—you felt lighter—happier?"

Linda nodded. She said:

"How did you know? That's just how I did feel."

Poirot said:

"Then do not repeat to yourself the imbecilities. Just make up your mind not to hate your next stepmother."

Linda said startled:

"Do you think I'm going to have another? Oh, I see, you mean Rosamund. I don't mind her." She hesitated a minute. "She's *sensible*."

It was not the adjective that Poirot himself would have selected for Rosamund Darnley, but he realised that it was Linda's idea of high praise.

3

Kenneth Marshall said:

"Rosamund, did you get some extraordinary idea into your head that I'd killed Arlena."

Rosamund looked rather shamefaced. She said:

"I suppose I was a damned fool."

"Of course you were."

"Yes, but Ken, you are such an oyster. I never knew what you really felt about Arlena. I didn't know if you accepted her as she was and were just frightfully decent about her, or whether you—well, just believed in her blindly. And I thought if it was that, and you suddenly found out that she was letting you down you might go mad with rage. I've heard stories about you. You're always very quiet but you're rather frightening sometimes."

"So you thought I just took her by the throat and throttled the life out of her?"

"Well—yes—that's just exactly what I did think. And your alibi seemed a bit on the light side. That's when I suddenly decided to take a hand, and made up that silly story about seeing you typing in your room. And when I heard that you said you'd seen me look in—well, that made me quite sure you'd done it. That, and Linda's queerness."

Kenneth Marshall said with a sigh:

"Don't you realise that I said I'd seen you in the mirror in order to back up *your* story. I—I thought you needed it corroborated."

Rosamund stared at him.

"You don't mean you thought that I killed your wife?"

Kenneth Marshall shifted uneasily. He mumbled:

"Dash it all, Rosamund, don't you remember how you nearly killed that boy about that dog once? How you hung on to his throat and wouldn't let go."

"But that was years ago."

"Yes, I know——"

Rosamund said sharply:

"What earthly motive do you think I had to kill Arlena?"

His glance shifted. He mumbled something again.

Rosamund cried:

" Ken, you mass of conceit! You thought I killed her out of altruism on your behalf, did you? Or—or did you think I killed her because I wanted you myself?"

" Not at all," said Kenneth Marshall indignantly. " But you know what you said that day—about Linda and everything—and—and you seemed to care what happened to me."

Rosamund said:

" I've always cared about that."

" I believe you have. You know, Rosamund—I can't usually talk about things—I'm not good at talking—but I'd like to get this clear. I didn't care for Arlena—only just a little at first—and living with her day after day was a pretty nerve-racking business. In fact it was absolute hell, but I *was* awfully sorry for her. She was such a damned fool— crazy about men—she just couldn't help it—and they always let her down and treated her rottenly. I simply felt I couldn't be the one to give her the final push. I'd married her and it was up to me to look after her as best I could. I think she knew that and was grateful to me really. She was— she was a pathetic sort of creature really."

Rosamund said gently:

" It's all right, Ken. I understand now."

Without looking at her Kenneth Marshall carefully filled a pipe. He mumbled:

" You're—pretty good at understanding, Rosamund."

A faint smile curved Rosamund's ironic mouth. She said:

" Are you going to ask me to marry you now, Ken, or are you determined to wait six months?"

Kenneth Marshall's pipe dropped from his lips and crashed on the rocks below.

He said:

" Damn, that's the second pipe I've lost down here. And I haven't got another with me. How the devil did you know I'd fixed six months as the proper time?"

" I suppose because it *is* the proper time. But I'd rather have something definite now, please. Because in the intervening months you may come across some other persecuted female and rush to the rescue in chivalrous fashion again."

He laughed.

" You're going to be the persecuted female this time, Rosamund. You're going to give up that damned dressmaking business of yours and we're going to live in the country."

"Don't you know that I make a very handsome income out of my business? Don't you realise that it's *My* business—that I created it and worked it up, and that I'm proud of it! And you've got the damned nerve to come along and say, ' Give it all up, dear.' "

"I've got the damned nerve to say it, yes."

"And you think I care enough for you to do it?"

"If you don't," said Kenneth Marshall, "you'd be no good to me."

Rosamund said softly:

"Oh, my dear, I've wanted to live in the country with you all my life. Now—it's going to come true. . . ."

THE END

Agatha Christie

The most popular and prolific writer of detective fiction ever known, her intricately plotted whodunits are enjoyed by armchair crime-solvers everywhere.

POIROT'S EARLY CASES 80p
SLEEPING MURDER 75p
CURTAIN: POIROT'S LAST CASE 75p
ORDEAL BY INNOCENCE 75p
N OR M? 75p
THE MIRROR CRACK'D FROM
  SIDE TO SIDE 75p
DEATH IN THE CLOUDS 75p
THE MURDER OF ROGER ACKROYD 75p
THE CLOCKS 75p
AT BERTRAM'S HOTEL 75p
FIVE LITTLE PIGS 75p
DESTINATION UNKNOWN 75p
MURDER ON THE ORIENT EXPRESS 75p
AFTER THE FUNERAL 75p
ENDLESS NIGHT 75p
DEATH ON THE NILE 80p

and many others

Fontana Paperbacks

Rex Stout

'His stories of Nero Wolfe, that amiable epicure, always provide excitement, wit, unflagging interest and ingenuity.' *Books of Today*. 'If there is anyone in the civilised world who is not acquainted with Nero Wolfe, Mr Stout's large, overbearing investigator, here is the opportunity to plug a shameful gap . . .' *Evening Standard*. 'It is impossible for Rex Stout to be anything but supremely readable.' *Guardian*

THE GOLDEN SPIDERS 75p
DEATH OF A DUDE 50p
A FAMILY AFFAIR 70p
TOO MANY COOKS 75p
THE FATHER HUNT 75p
IF DEATH EVER SLEPT 80p
SOME BURIED CAESAR 80p

Fontana Paperbacks

Fontana Paperbacks

Fontana is a leading paperback publisher of fiction and non-fiction, with authors ranging from Alistair MacLean, Agatha Christie and Desmond Bagley to Solzhenitsyn and Pasternak, from Gerald Durrell and Joy Adamson to the famous Modern Masters series.

In addition to a wide-ranging collection of internationally popular writers of fiction, Fontana also has an outstanding reputation for history, natural history, military history, psychology, psychiatry, politics, economics, religion and the social sciences.

All Fontana books are available at your bookshop or newsagent; or can be ordered direct. Just fill in the form and list the titles you want.

_____

FONTANA BOOKS, Cash Sales Department, G.P.O. Box 29, Douglas, Isle of Man, British Isles. Please send purchase price, plus 8p per book. Customers outside the U.K. send purchase price, plus 10p per book. Cheque, postal or money order. No currency.

NAME (Block letters)

_____

ADDRESS

_____

_____

_____